Open

Your

Eyes

Open Your Eyes

Paul Jessup

AN APEX PUBLICATIONS BOOK
Lexington, Kentucky

Published by Apex Publications, LLC
PO Box 24323
Lexington, KY 40524

www.apexbookcompany.com
www.pauljessup.com
www.danielecascone.com
www.jdavidsonartworks.com

First Edition, April 2009

ISBN: 978-0-9821596-0-6

Printed in the United States of America

10 9 8 7 6 5 4 3 2 1

A special thanks to everyone involved in the making of this book. Thanks to my mom and dad for pushing me when I needed to be pushed and being there for me when I needed it. Thanks to my wife, Rachel, for putting up with my crazies, and to my two kids, Liam and Ashlyn, for being my muse and inspiration. Thanks also to my grandparents, my brothers and sisters, and my in-laws for being awesome and supportive of my endeavors. I would never have gotten as far as I have without a family as large and amazing as this. Thank you everyone. One last thank you goes out to Jonathan Wood, Sam Taylor, Michelle Muenzler, Rosa Weber, and Alex Dally MacFarlane for being awesome first readers.

I

Her lover was a supernova. She smiled when he came, his bright burning light rocking her body, impregnating her with the essence of stars. Through the metal bones of her ship she felt the gasses enter her, felt the compound light exploding inside her. Her hands clawed at the cracked vinyl of the chair, her legs spread to either side with toes stretched out, her mouth in piercing screams of ecstasy.

Her lover was a supernova. And her womb—it spun with the light of stars. She felt black holes open up inside of her, intense gravitational weight. She felt her mind expand, and then a stillness as the blue light glowed and everything around her was awash in a sea of colors.

She couldn't make out the controls. Not now. Not even in her mind. She lay back and let the ship fly itself, a small vessel in the starsea, floating through the explosions around her. Everything sucked in, the large mass pulling in stars and planets and satellites and docking stations and floating flophouses.

Ekhi saw the sun center of her lover and felt herself push through to the other side, her eyes half lidded in rapture, her warm hands on the smooth, round flesh of her stomach, rubbing in circles the home of a new galaxy, of a new starling landscape growing inside of her.

They vaulted outward, the boneship starspat and spinning, the lights inside of the crusted and cracked marrow cage blistering with warning signs. She came as they forced their way out, howling alive on the other side, her eyes rolling in her head like marble spheres as she gasped in the glory of orgasm. The lights dimmed into a slow halo glow of amber, blue, and then out. Exhaled. Like a candle flame.

The engines wound down. The seconds unticked. She felt time unravel inside the great ribcage of her egia. The great body of the ship was losing power, the few orange lights still active only flashing mute warning signs.

Adrift, her displays dead, her radios silenced. Everything in the ship shut down and shut off. Not enough fuel to get home. Just energy enough to drift and make oxygen, keeping her alive in the empty void of space for a few more months. The oxygen vents around her wheezed in and out, conserving as much energy as possible as they tried to keep her alive, tried to stave off the empty void of space for one more moment.

She sighed and trembled, her finger to her lip as her nerves burst in radial songs of joy and adulation. Her body floated up, the artificial gravity turned off to save power. Behind her the light of the nova shined on, bright and brighter still. *My lover is dying*, she thought, *and he's taking out whole worlds with him.*

Ekhi smiled and sung a lullaby to herself, the whole of space immaculate with her lover's last breath, the stars growing dimmer by each moment.

II

Lights. Circles moved over ripped vinyl chairs and cracked

bone ceilings. Yellow halos dipped on instrument panels, searching for anything of value. Air was thin. Oxygen tanks exhaled their last few breaths. Three figures walked through dark and shadowy ribs, each one with an electric lantern that gave off a cold, yellow circle of light.

Scavengers. Airtight chitinous armor clung to their bodies. Breathing masks covered their faces and clicked with animatronic mandibles. Like spiders they crawled through the egia, searching for anything they could pillage.

One figure shined a light over a body that floated in the middle of the hallway, suspended above a chair that had tears along the armrests with clouds of cotton puffing through. The body was nude and female; her eyes were closed in slits of sleep. She snored as she spun, her bare breasts suspended in zero gravity. The yellow circle focused on her body, moving up her toes, up her legs, up her thighs.

A voice from an insect armor. Male. "Well fuck. I think we hit the jackpot."

The other insects turned and looked. Their numen suits gleamed in the darkness of space, their eyes lit blue and human beyond the clear shell of the insect masks. "Damn, Hodei. What you find?"

"What do you think? She looks like she's been out only a little bit. Oxygen reads that it has only been thin for a few hours. Probably very little brain damage, if any. We came just in the nick of time."

A crackling of static filled the helmets, and then a whisper of words that sounded like two stones rubbing together. The Captain, a ghost in their terminal, a spirit watching over them from afar.

A female voice from the third insect, one demanding respect: "Captain says we're taking her on board the ship. Leaving her here to die would be unethical. We bring her back to the egia, and then come back to scavenge for supplies. Got it?"

The yellow moon moved away from the floating body and focused on the bone structure of the ship. Eyes followed the light. "Look at this place—all the foodstuff has been vaporized. Nothing but dust. And it's off the chart for radioactivity. The walls, the shelves, everything is still hot to the touch. I'm starting to think we're going to get nothing but her out of this."

The one called Hodei walked toward the floating body. He held a gloved hand over an ankle, framing it with his clicking arachnid fingers. "She's so beautiful."

The female insect walked forward with a marionette gait, her magnetic steps sending out loud clanging echoes as she brought out a weapon resembling a scorpion's tail.

The betadur was segmented, and the segments were filled with sparkling blue light. The tip glowed a bright orange, and the air tensed around it with a sparkling symmetry. "Hodei, please. Let's just move her into the ship. Waking her up here could be disastrous. We don't know what happened to her just yet. She could be in shock."

He moved his hand away, staring still at the barrel of the betadur. "No problem."

She sighed. "Sugoi, help me move this girl back to our

egia. Hodei, you stay here and scavenge. Make sure we leave nothing behind."

Hodei sighed and watched the two of them walk up to the naked body and gently nudge it toward the rear docking vents. The body spun violently as it floated, the arms out to either side making circles in the air as she corkscrewed toward the exit. Her shoulder-length black hair puffed up like a messy halo over her head.

The cold lantern lights shone against her brown skin, reflected against the dented bone walls behind them. Hodei walked over to the dead instrument panel, hiding his face and obscuring his features, muttering obscenities to himself.

III

Cotton cocoon. Ekhi struggled inside of it, pushing her head through the tightening layers of fabric to look around. Outside of the cocoon: steel bunk beds, bone ceiling. Circles of painful orange lights shedding amber shadows. Her head throbbed and her body ached. Ekhi could not remember why she hurt, did not know where she was. She only remembered the blue light of her lover and the greatest sensation she had ever felt, a volcanic eruption of orgasm after orgasm.

The room was cramped with metallic furniture. Chairs and tables and beds crowded around one another in a chaotic disharmony. Cards lay spat and scattered across the floor, their pixilated surfaces displaying heroic figures and brutal images of war.

Beside a rusty circular door, sat a woman reading a cracked leather book that lay flat against her lap. Her face was half gone, replaced by a silver latticework that made a cage out of her skull. The eye on her left side was a red jewel sparkling in the halogen lights. Inside the metal cage of her face fluttered two mechanical butterflies, their wings shedding rainbows of refracted colors.

Ekhi gasped in surprise.

The flesh half of the woman's face twisted into a sweet smile. The metallic half stayed still, the only motion that of the butterflies that whirred around inside of her skull. "Morning," she said.

Ekhi nodded. "Morning?"

The woman shrugged. "It's always morning somewhere."

Ekhi looked down at her hands. She was naked beneath the blanket. She felt vulnerable and hated the feeling. It left a bitter taste in her mouth. "Oh," she said, "I guess so."

The woman looked down at her book. She stared at the page for a moment, and then marked it with a thin piece of newspaper that made a crinkling noise as she closed the book slowly, sighing. "My name is Mari. Welcome aboard the Good Ship Lollipop."

Ekhi stared at the knuckles on her hands. They grasped the blanket hard enough to turn red. Ekhi knew that there was a joke in what Mari said, but could not find the cultural reference in order to process it. "My name," she said, searching her mind for the meaning behind herself, "Is Ekhi. Do you..."

She paused, looking harder at her knuckles and the twisted knots of cotton below them. "Do you know why I'm here?"

Mari put her book on the ground and walked over to the bunk bed, sitting on the edge. Her good eye looked at Ekhi. It was like a grey metal ball floating in a sea of milk. Her hair was also grey, but not an aged grey. A metallic grey. An accent to the machine part of her face.

"That's an easy one. We saw your ship floating amongst all this debris and we latched on to it. We were going to scavenge it for food and maybe some cash, but, well, all we found was you. Why were you out there, floating naked? And why was everything inside your egia destroyed? We don't have answers for that. We were hoping you would."

Ekhi pulled the cotton cocoon up over her breasts, concealing herself again as the round door creaked open. A boy stood at the door, probably no older than eighteen. His hair was a mess of disheveled black curls and his thin brown face had a carved stone quality. He puffed his lips out, pouting as he talked. "Mari, she up finally?"

He turned and saw Ekhi and winked. "She is! How's my sleeping beauty doing? Let's say you and me take a tour of all the dark corners of the ship. I'll show you why I'm wanted in fourteen galaxies, and why my face is plastered on all the tabloids as the sexiest bachelor in space."

Ekhi shook her head, trying hard not to let the blanket droop down. The boy stared at the curves of flesh that peeked out from the top of the fabric, his gaze intent on making the blanket fall down with the power of his mind. "No thanks," she said.

He shrugged. "Your loss. But in a few weeks, when the lonely void starts eating at you and you need some comfort, I will be here, waiting. To comfort you. Physically."

Mari walked up and hit him over the head with the back of her hand. His head whipped forward in pain, his hair dancing around either side of his skull. "Ow, fuck." He rubbed the back of his head. "What did you do that for?"

"She's a guest, jackass, that's why. Ekhi, this is Hodei. Our in-ship mechanic, space scavenger extraordinaire, petty thief, and resident pervert."

Hodei bowed and smiled. "At your service, madam. If you need anything—oh, and I mean *anything*—just let me know, and I will be more than happy to assist. More. Than. Happy."

Mari shoved him out the door, and then turned to Ekhi, her metal face glittering. "The captain will want to see you soon. I'll let her know that you're awake and ready to talk."

IV

Coils of black and gold cords unwrapped, stretched out, pushed forward. A fogged-over glass chamber swung open, gold leaf and vine decorations coating the top and bottom. Between the nests of wires and cords lay blinking artificial stars, multicolored lights giving out complex information matrices discernable only to a trained mechanical eye.

Pushing out of this electric womb was a young girl, probably no older than twelve. Her skin was the color of pale melted wax, her eyes like glass balls with painted irises in the center. Her hair coiled in blue curls, the cords and wires wrapped up in the mess of her tresses. She wore a black lacey dress that puffed out like an umbrella. On her legs and her arms were green and black striped stockings.

Her eyes blinked. They sounded like a camera lens. Opening, closing. "Welcome aboard my ship."

Ekhi's back was against another round door, the rusted orange metal staining her shirt. To her left and right the bone walls rested, breathing. "Thank you," she said.

"You know, we could've left you for dead."

A statement like a knife under her ribs.

Ekhi sighed and looked at her feet. Her legs and ankles and toes were still bare. They had given her a long grey shirt to wear, one that barely covered her body when she moved. She felt the boys stare at her with each gesture, waiting for the raise of an arm or a leg that would reveal her secrets to them.

The doll girl walked forward, pulling the cables from her body. "You have nothing to worry about here. I just bring up the point so that you understand your situation. So you understand that you mean nothing to us."

Ekhi looked into the girl's face. It appeared artificial,

like a mask. It gave her an uncanny feeling of a ghost haunting a puppet. "I understand," she muttered.

The doll girl tilted her head to the side. She smiled, her teeth lined with sparkling electrodes. "Good, good. We can use some help on this ship. What do you know about egias?"

Ekhi instinctively raised her hand to her belly. She felt the growth inside of her—gasses compacting into mass, stars whirling around, chinks of rock aligning into orbit and gravities pulling and yanking inside her womb. "Quite a bit. I piloted my own egia for several years. Without any sentient servants of any sort. The ship didn't even have a heart. I piloted the thing bare, to the bone. Flying straight and naked in space."

The doll paused, her eyes slit with thought. "Hmm. Well, we have a heart and a crew on this ship. This isn't some small thing, some tiny space vessel. We could use someone with the knowledge, but you have to remember that I am in charge here. Not you. Not anyone else. The walls of this ship are paper thin, barely keeping away the painful void of space. It would be so easy to push you through those walls, push you out into a grave of stars. Understand?"

"Yes," Ekhi said. Her chest tightened into a knot; her lungs entangled around each other, slipping over the valves of her heart. She knew that she had no choice.

The doll sighed. "Now then. Have you any questions for me?"

Ekhi paused. "No."

The doll shrugged. "My name is Itsasu. Aren't you at least curious as to where we are going, what we are doing?"

Ekhi remembered the gasses of her lover surrounding her. She remembered her arms grasping and clawing at the vinyl chair. She remembered that feeling, that wonderful feeling, and everything around her paled in comparison. "No," she answered. "No. I guess I'm not."

The doll smiled. "Good. We'll get along just fine. You are such a curious specimen of humanity."

V

A relic, Itsasu thought. This flesh is a relic.

She breathed in the fluid and felt like she was drowning. It wasn't painful. Not anymore. But she remembered the first time she had been submerged in the preservation tank. Fire had filled her. Fire had consumed her. And thunder. Her breath had been thunder.

She watched a flickering image of Mari wander through the halls of the egia, projected onto the amber holograph fluid. Mari's muscles stretched with each movement, the silver hair dancing around her head. Mari's arms swung back and forth as she walked, meat pendulums that teased Itsasu with their solidity and strength.

Itsasu stared at the moving body, zoomed in on each tendon stretching and flexing. She felt a tingling along her bent legs, a tingling in her mouth and a growing heat in her body. Itsasu moved her head in closer through the

gelatinous prison, her eye touching the hologram, caress-
ing it. She licked the figure, the tingling balls of firefly light
coating her taste buds as she ran her tongue over the image of the muscular meat face. The hologram blurred and
shook at the movement, disturbed by the rocking fluids.

Itsasu's twig arms twisted about, trying to reach down
and pleasure her, the gnarled limbs unable to do more
than reach across her stomach. The egia, sensing her
need, sent pleasure chemicals through the water. She
smiled a maniacal grin and dreamt of Mari's flesh for herself. She dreamt of strong bones untouched by age and
no longer made brittle by the lasting centuries. She
dreamt of skin no longer paper thin, but supple and
gripped with muscles. She dreamt of dancing with her
husband, back before the war took him, before she had
been left stranded in the ancient planets, searching the
alien ruins for a way to bring him back to life.

She gurgled and dreamt, the lazy light of blue suns
glinting on the bones of her ship.

VI

Hodei sat on a moon-shaped chair and sipped hot coffee
from a black bulb. His brown fingers grasped the sides,
feeling the warmth against his hands. He perused a
magazine in his lap, his eyes browsing over the slick
pages of women in different stages of undress and
arousal. The texture of the paper against his hand was
like flesh, real and smooth and clean.

It wasn't the nudity that kept him coming to this magazine at each port. It was a specific girl. The nets had no info on her, none that he could find. But there she was, a ghost of space. A haunting female form that burned itself into the landscape of his mind.

His first glimpse of her had been a stark and beautiful memory that haunted his dreaming hours. She had been just a background figure in revealing white robes, shaved legs dangling beneath, her hips and waist barely covered. Her red hair contrasted her pale face like scarlet blades to either side of a white cloth; her mouth formed a thick-lipped, mischievous smile. There was something in her eyes that pulled him in. A restless yearning. A desire for something greater. Even though she had four pages of revealing nudity, her eyes and her lips and her face were what brought him back, made him search her out. She was not just another model. Her presence was more jovial, more jocular, more searching and burning.

"Hey cowboy, find any good cattle?"

Startled, Hodei looked up and saw Mari staring at him. Her one good eye was an intense beam of light; her jeweled eye offered him no solace from her angry gaze.

"Cattle? Cute, Mari. Cute. Not sure if she's in this one. I haven't seen her in the last two issues. I hope she's all right. What's gotten into you?"

Mari walked over to the coffee maker and flipped a cracked switch. The machine whirred to life, grinding beans into a fine powder and boiling water in a draconian hiss. "It's your idiot brother, is all."

Hodei raised an eyebrow. He sat up, concerned. "Trouble in paradise? Knew you two wouldn't work out. He's too stupid for you. I told you that a long time ago. Sugoi, he's different in a bad kinda way, you know? He didn't even go to school. He flunked out before anything stuck, and now his brain is like antimatter, destroying any knowledge that tries to approach it."

He gently closed the magazine, then slid it into the drawer behind him, making sure not to crease or bend the delicate pages. Later, he would get a small plastic bag and gently slide the magazine in, labeling the outside and storing it in deep freeze with the others. His library. His most precious possession.

"Not like me," he said almost casually, "I mean, I don't show it, but I'm pretty smart."

Mari coughed, trying to hold back a laugh. Hodei looked at the ground, covering up his embarrassment. "Hey, that's not nice. I may not be a brute, but I got my own benefits, you know."

Mari sighed when she realized he was serious. "I don't even know why I come to you to talk. Look, just because we're having problems doesn't mean I'm going to leave him for you. I love your brother, even in his flaws. We've been together for four years. One little mistake isn't going to change that."

Hodei looked up, his face red and his expression a mix of anger and sorrow. "All right then. So what is it? What did my big brother do that was so damned horrible?"

"It's not. I mean it is. Well, damnit. He's just distant as

of late, you know? And he keeps looking at that new girl. Fuck. It's like I don't even exist sometimes. He'll just stare at her, and all of a sudden I'm not there anymore. I'm just a transparent thing. And I don't like that. You know?"

Hodei grinned. "She is hot, all right."

Mari walked over and punched him in the arm, leaving a small bruise beneath his jumper. "Aw, fuck, why'd you go and hit me for? It's not my fault that some pretty new thing turns his head."

"You're no help, you know that?"

Hodei shrugged. "More than the captain. She would just give you some bullshit line, spoken through one of those dolls. About ethics in space. About no sex on the egia. That sort of thing. Me, well, at least I'm still flesh and blood, you know? The machine and void haven't eaten me away just yet. I still got sex on the mind, and I can relate."

He sighed and leaned back. "Besides. What do you want me to do or say anyway?"

She sat down on the chair. The hissing stopped and the smell of freshly brewed coffee filled the air as the room once again fell silent. She reached over and grabbed her own bulb of coffee, her hands almost burning from the heat. Her features were slack, emotionless. "I don't know, Hodei. I don't know. Maybe...maybe you can talk to him. Ask him what he feels, you know? Get him to tell you the situation."

Hodei laughed, hard and loud, like a seal. His voice echoed in the chamber; his laughter bounced off the ribs and absorbed into the orange padding. "Oh man, you want me to go up to my brother and ask him about his love life? To get him to what? Open up to me? That's rich! What the hell do you think I am? Huh? I'm his baby brother. If I say shit like that, he'll beat the fuck out of me and you know it."

Mari frowned. The metal side of her face stayed emotionless, the butterflies in flight calming down, resting on the silver cage, no longer refracting rainbows of light. "You're right. But it's my only hope. What the hell am I supposed to do?"

Hodei beat his fist into his hand. "Punch him. He won't hit you back—you're his girl. And if he even thinks about it, he knows that the captain will be watching and he'll be shoved out into the void if he lays a hand on you. If he asks you why you hit him, you tell him you'll do it again, at random points during the day. That way he'll have to watch you, just so he can see when it's coming. He will have to pay attention to you then."

Mari sipped her coffee, looking at Hodei over the ceramic lips of the bulb. "You're a fucking idiot, you know that? Just see if you can talk to him. I don't care if he hits you for it. If you don't, I'll hit you. And what would the great space bachelor Hodei do if at every port they knew he got beat up by some half metal woman?"

Hodei stared at the padded walls in silence for a moment. He then stood up, looking at the ground. His face tried to betray emotions—so many complex emotions—but he held them in, keeping them behind a twisted map of his face. He threw his bulb against the wall. Coffee sprayed across the floor, the bulb bounced against the padding and then dropped to the floor—clink clink clink. He stormed out, not saying a word. Mari smiled and knew that she would be getting her information soon enough.

VII

Hodei paced in the engine room, knotted metal and brass wires brushing against his jumper, soft firefly sparks pulsating as they jerked and hovered in the air. In the center of the room sat giant wet eggs, quivering and green and covered in sparkling electric webbing and film. In the center of the eggs nested the entanglement engine.

The engine resembled a human skull, bigger than Hodei, bigger than even Sugoi. It was yellowed with age, cracks lining different pieces glued back together by the competent hands of the mozorro. It took up the width of the hallway, the eye sockets lined with translucent fungal wires.

Behind him, Hodei heard the door slide open with a loud clang, and then footsteps. Sugoi, he thought. Just on time. Acting like he had nothing planned, Hodei leaned in to get a closer look at the entanglement engine. He heard whispers in the skull, strange psychotic words that crossed over each other, a hundred voices, each of them mad. Conversations of ghosts. Each of them centuries gone, each of them trapped inside the engine, powering it.

He felt a stone hand on his shoulder. The fingers bit into his bone. "Hey. You. What you say? Huh? You say mean?"

Hodei didn't turn around. "What are you talking about?"

Sugoi moaned. "What? What. I tell. Mari, she mad for something. Dunno what. Last I saw, you talk her. Then I get you note. Come to ungun room. So I come. What? What you say her? What you *do* her? Huh? You tell. I listen. Now."

Hodei sighed. He heard the song of dead worlds, sung in the voices of ghost children. He heard stories of century-long wars fought in the void of space, with junk graves floating like asteroid belts around a wounded sun. "Look, dumbass, she was making fun of me for my porn."

Laughter. The hand loosened, then patted him hard on the back. Hodei realized it was okay to turn around. His brother no longer saw him as a threat. The last time he had been seen as a threat he spent a week in bed, the thalna combing over his body with their little hands, stitching him slowly back to life.

Sugoi was twice Hodei's height, with a head that scraped on the ribs of the ceiling, his eyes black stones in his skull. *A giant*, Hodei thought. *My brother is a giant carved out of stone.*

"You stop reading that stuff. No thing for real girl. And we got new one now. You like, eh?"

Hodei smiled. He could use this conversation after all. "Yeah, she is hot. What do you think, you think I got a chance?"

Sugoi shrugged. If he had been a mountain, the sky would have been filled with moving stone. "Not your type, brotherbaby."

Hodei felt his tools along his belt. He would need something, in case Sugoi got mad. He wasn't going in un-armed again. The screwdriver should do in a pinch. The wrong word, the wrong phrase, and his brother would erupt into violence. "I'm not? Well, whose type is she?"

Sugoi leaned his arms on his knees, just so he was eye level with his little brother. The giant smelled of dirt. Of trees and moss. The stone lips opened and spoke, his words the sealing of a grave. "She my type."

Hodei leaned back and wrapped his fingers around the handle of the screwdriver. "I thought, well, I thought Mari was your type."

Sugoi laughed. "She is. They both my type. But you can have other girl. Just want seconds, you know? I even help. Good for both, you know? We share when you get."

Hodei forced a laugh. "Yeah. Sure. Whatever you say, big brother."

VIII

The mozorro cleaned. They climbed the halls of the egia, their nimble hands and legs digging into the giant bone architecture, latching onto ceiling, wall, and floor with me-chanical agility. Their clay skin glittered with a microscopic intelligent dust, reading radio waves from Itsasu's cage in the heart of the ship, recording their movements and sending them back to her for approval.

Their lizard-bone skulls swerved around with ratcheting sounds, pastel lenses deep in their eye sockets looking at each object they touched, inspecting it for flaws or anything that could be collected into a databank and marked with metatags.

They read back data as they scrubbed and fixed and cleaned, a constant stream of information, a societal memory that flowed with the ticking of the seconds. Notes and tags and images danced about, creating new formations, new layers within each mozorro as they hunted through the ship. The data danced into probabilities, the probabilities became predictions, and the mozorro prepared for and awaited each catastrophe with an all-seeing prescience, using all of their abilities to keep the egia running and its crew alive.

IX

Itsasu watched with mozorro eyes as Mari walked into the engine room. Itsasu's crippled body swam around in her fluid, her frail form tensing. Her lips twisted back into a grin, a struggle for her skin and bones.

She watched as Mari walked over to one of the low-burning ion drives and ran her hand over the twisted, sparkling cages. The metal half of her face flashed dimly as she smiled and ran her fingers close to the firefly lights. Around the engine skull crawled several mozorro, scrubbing and cleaning and fixing to perfection.

Another mozorro crawled across the ceiling, focusing on a brown body walking into the engine room. The dusty suit of Sugoi, his face twitching, his hair mussed up on his head. Itsasu swam closer, her eye as close to the holo as possible. She clenched her bony fists to her sides and felt the fragile skin breaking with each movement, her blood a red dust in the fluid.

"The ungun room popular. For me. Why we meet here? Not in rooms? Like normals?"

Mari turned. Itsasu noticed the way Mari hid her face, trying to put the metal side in shadows as much as possible. "I need to talk to you. About the new girl. Why is she still here? We should've just sent her out in the pod or something."

Sugoi shrugged. His eyes glanced at the whirring metal cages and the turning wire cords, his face struggling to hide a smirk at the mention of the new girl. "Dunno. You know captain. She got plans, sure. Hodei likes Ekhi enough."

Mari walked forward, still hidden by the shadows. The only hint of her metallic face was the whirring of butterflies reflecting firefly lights. "Your brother likes anything with legs."

Sugoi paused, staring at her. His eyes glared at the shadows, trying to see the metallic half of her face. "He not like you."

She smiled, her good eye darting over his massive body. His whole form was retracted inward and tensed to snapping. Her red jewel reflected engine light in the darkness, a sparkling black amongst the shadows. "Never stopped him from hitting on me before."

Sugoi's eyes glinted, emotion breaking through the stone façade, a visage of slow pain. Anger and heat rose up inside his eyes, until they closed into slits of frustration. "I will break. Break bones. Break all. He lie. Lie to me."

Mari stepped back. Such violence, about ready to spring from the massive body.

"Trust him. He didn't hit on me recently. I was talking about before."

Sugoi chuckled. "Yeah. Still."

Itsasu licked her lips, her eyes narrowing as she glanced over the holos, her eyes tracing his muscles. She zoomed in on Sugoi's face, looking at each muscle in his jaw as he spoke. The flexing of the skin, the raw stubble across his cheek. Itsasu felt warm again, excited again.

Itsasu watched a smooth hand touch that cheek. One stained with grease. Mari's hand? Manicured. Mari's voice entered Itsasu's gelatin prison. "Sugoi. Listen to me. The captain's mission is important to us all, right?"

A pause. Heavy breathing. The hand moved off the cheek. The cheekbones were smooth. Itsasu could see every pore and blemish on that wonderful young flesh. "Yeah."

"I mean, you still believe in our fearless leader, right?"

A shrug. Barely perceptible from this close. Itsasu saw muscles tensing, relaxing. She felt her own body tense, her whole frail form tighten. Her legs and groin tingled with a fluttering sensation. She resisted the urge to flail her twig limbs, resisted the need to unwrap her claw hands and try to reach down once again.

"Sure I do."

Each word was a muscle clenching, releasing, clenching, releasing.

"I do too. But I have this feeling that, well, that this new passenger is going to change things. Maybe even derail the mission. And where would that leave us? Us and all those years we spent on this ship, searching for—"

A pause.

"Don't say, Mari. If you right, then we quiet. Not speak."

Strands of braided hair moved over the camera. Gun grey hair. Itsasu cursed and switched to a different mozorro. She saw the flesh of a bare back, curved hips and a straight spine. The metal face was no longer hidden by shadows, but instead stood vulnerable in the engine light, the butterflies beneath her skull cage dancing about in frenzied intensity. When had Mari dropped her clothes? "You're right. Let's do this quick, before your brother comes looking for us."

Her back muscles flexed as Sugoi unzipped his dirty jumper and let it pool on the floor in a dusty heap. Several mozorro scurried up and cleaned around his clothes, making sure not to disturb the loose pile of fabric.

Mari walked over to Sugoi, leaned in and kissed him across his chest, pushing him to the floor as his hands tangled up in her grey hair. The sound of the engine became a thundering rush of sounds as Mari straddled him, her hands on his chest as her back muscles tensed, released and tensed again.

Itsasu could not restrain herself anymore. She flailed her limbs, her arms down. She heard the snapping of her arm breaking and cursed as the pleasure fluids entered her prison once again.

She groaned in frustration and pleasure. It wasn't the same, not without the physical contact. Even masturbation was something. This—this chemical love was unsatisfying. She flailed and moaned and came in conjunction with Mari and Sugoi, three rigid bodies releasing themselves in the floating graveyard of space.

X

Ekhi flailed against the walls, a mad ghost wailing in the honeycombed halls. Her mouth frantically formed shapes, her lips twisted and grimaced with each howling scream. She clawed at her shirt, her skin, clawed as if something was living beneath her skin and she had to dig it out. She had ripped and torn her face; her fingernails were still clogged with tiny bits of flesh and blood.

Down the hall, Mari ran toward the screams with Sugoi behind her; they were both red-faced and sweating, their minds buzzing with after-sex endorphins. They followed the panicked mozorro that scrambled and clung to the walls, not ready to see the broken figure of Ekhi in a complete and total psychotic break.

At the other end of the hallway ran Hodei, his eyes large and panicked, his hands pumping to either side. He did not make any sound as he ran, his footsteps swallowed by her screams.

Ekhi was trapped. The walls rushed in, the bodies rushed in. She tried to form words in her screams, tried to turn her cries into an expression of her dread and emptiness so the others could understand her pain, so the walls would feel empathy and not smother her underneath their honey limbs.

Mari reached her first, holding her, putting the screaming head against the smooth skin of her chest. Ekhi heard Mari's heart beating like a clock planted between rib bones. Mari's eyes closed as she said incantations under her breath, trying by her will alone to make all of this stop, make Ekhi become normal once again. In response, Ekhi sobbed and rubbed her head up against Mari's shoulder, her tears mixing with the sweat of sex.

"He's dead!" Ekhi screamed, her voice muffled by breasts and shirt.

Hodei crouched down, putting a hand on Mari's shoulder, his fingers resting against bare skin, the metal cage of her cheek brushing against his knuckles. A spark of connection, a sadness flowed through the three of them like an open circuit. They saw the nova, felt the rising force of orgasms, and shivered intimately. The death of a star. The birth of a galaxy.

Sugoi shot his brother a warning glance, a threatening stare. Hodei shrugged, but did not move his hand. Ekhi screamed. "He went nova, nova, nova. He took out so many planets and neighboring stars. But not me. Not me. Why am I still alive? Why am I still here? I want to be dead! Why can't I be dead? Why am I left behind?"

Mari tried to think of something appropriate to say. She could think of nothing at all. So instead she chanted more calming words under her breath, the phrases like steel rods rubbing together as she ran her hands through Ekhi's hair. Ekhi screamed and wailed and bit and pushed, painful hands on breastbone, knees digging into ribs, teeth pushing past flesh and leaving red moons on Mari's arm. Mari said nothing but her incantation, biting back her own screams of pain.

Sugoi stomped over to Hodei, his fists clenched and his eyes burning. He said something that was lost amongst the screams. Something threatening to Hodei. A warning, perhaps. Or a threat of things to come. His voice was low. It rumbled beneath the ship like an asteroid striking the armored sides, a thunder in the halls.

Hodei said nothing. He stood his ground, staring at his brother, the threats hitting hard and deep but causing no damage. Mari did not know what was happening. All she knew was that Ekhi screamed and Ekhi remembered, and that Mari would hate to be in that situation. To see Sugoi die before her very eyes. To be a survivor, carrying their child inside, planted with memories and genetic architecture, but still alone, haunted by the moments they had spent together.

Sugoi tensed, his rock form trembling. He pushed Hodei

to the ground, the massive force throwing his tiny brother across the room with a single flick of a finger. Mari saw and could not move. She screamed "*stop*," but it was lost amongst the wails and the sobs and combat, her words floating empty, without meaning, formless spirits forced back into the ether without purpose.

Hodei stood up, whipping out a crowbar from behind his back. It shone black under the halos of orange light.

STOP! STOP! He's dead! He's dead! screamed Ekhi. *I will never see him again! Stop! Please stop. Stop it. Don't kill each other—bring him back to life! Take me beyond death! I can't handle this anymore. I can't. Please stop. Don't do this. We don't need this. Stop.*

Footsteps. In the hall. Clanging, metallic. The footsteps of a doll. Hodei turned to see who it was, the ripples of his spine exposed. Sugoi moved a giant stone fist, punching Hodei square in the back as one of Itsasu's dolls glided into the far end of the hall. Hodei's body hit the ground with a wet thump.

Around Itsasu's blue-haired doll floated the thalna on lightning-coated wings, their little eyes glowing blue with a holy neon light that blinked in short bursts of electrical conversation. Hodei spasmed on the ground in front of her, Sugoi grinning over his body like a mad giant about ready to eat for the first time in months.

Ekhi stopped screaming when she saw the captain's doll. She lay quietly, curled up in Mari's arms, gnawing tiny mouse holes in her fingers with the pointed tips of her eyeteeth.

Several of the thalna flew down and stitched Hodei back together, webs of glowing light fluttering beneath their fingers and sticking to his wet skin with a faint scratching sound, like a knife against canvas removing paint. Sugoi stepped back, letting the doll through. She did not say anything to him. Not a word of reprimand or appraisal.

She bent over, her doll eyes staring into Ekhi's flushed face. "I see that you remember."

Ekhi nodded, muttering incantations under her breath.

"Good. Do you want to forget him? Your lover? Forever? I can do it. One word and the thalna will enter your mind, fixing it forever with their tiny scalpels. Is that what you want?"

Ekhi shook her head. "I have a responsibility. To remember him. For my sake. For our daughter's sake."

The doll nodded. "I understand. Do you want a sedative?"

Ekhi smiled. "No, no I'm fine now. A little shaken. But that's about it."

Mari helped Ekhi stand. Marble eyes watched them move, recording each movement and sending it back to Itsasu through her doll. Sugoi stood and watched as well, waiting for them to leave. Waiting to be alone with Hodei once again. So he could break him, smash him, grind his face into the ribs of the egia for touching his girl.

The two women walked down the hallway, arms around each other's waists, each using the other for support. They were like dolls themselves, broken rag dolls, trying to prop up one another's boneless bodies. Itsasu watched through avatar eyes, through the mozorro eyes, through a thousand many-faceted eyes throughout the ship. The doll did not move her head, her face still staring down the hall. She whispered back to Sugoi, who waited.

"You had better go. Go back to your room. I'll take good care of your brother. Understand?"

Sugoi did not nod, did not respond verbally. He only turned and walked back down the long ribs of the hallway. He would deal with Hodei later. He kept such events logged in his mind, deep in the crevices of his hate-drenched soul.

Someday he was going to kill his brother.

It was just a matter of time.

XI

Ekhi sat on her bed, the soft sheets knotted around her waist and legs, and a bulb of tea between her hands. Her eyes closed as the aroma of it teased her senses. Mari sat in the same chair by the same round door, a replica of when Ekhi had first awakened on board this new egia.

Maybe I was sleepwalking, Ekhi thought as she sipped the tea, the steam tickling her nose. *Maybe I was sleep-walking and I just woke up now. That is why all of this is the same. Because now, now I am really awake.*

Mari sighed, then spoke. Her voice was naked, the only sound in the room. "We're hitting a port tomorrow. Floating port, out in the void of space. You don't have to

stay with us. You could find someone else there. Someone else who could take you—"

Ekhi opened her eyes. She was calm. A strange calm.
The orange lights were low, tinting the room amber. "No,"
Ekhi said, "What would I do? He's not there anymore."

Mari nodded. "You want me to go? I can leave you
alone now, if you would like."

Ekhi sipped some more tea. Calm. No, she wasn't
calm. That was the wrong word for this. Numb. She was
numb. "No," she said, "I want you to stay."

Mari walked over and sat on the edge of her bed.
"Okay. But I have to warn you, I'm not good company. I
guess that's why me and Sugoi are perfect together. He
doesn't talk, and he doesn't expect me too, either."

The tea tasted strange on her tongue. Like a forest
fire. As if Mari's words had corrupted its flavor. "I know. I
mean, in a way. I know."

Mari pulled Ekhi against her shoulder again. "It's the
same isn't it? Both of us trapped in silence. Silence we
enjoy. What do you plan on naming her, your daughter?"

Ekhi sighed. "I don't know. I don't even know her yet.
I'm not even starting to show. Maybe then, when I'm bal-
looning out and this *feels* real, when it is concrete fact.
Then I can come up with a name for her."

Mari kissed Ekhi on the head, her hair brushing
against Ekhi's lips and teeth. "Nothing is ever concrete."

Their voices died down, their breaths silent in their
lips. No noise, no sound. Not even the struggling engines
of the ship or the cleaning of the mozorro. Just a void of

space engulfing them with non-noise, surrounding them with non-being.

XII

Ekhi awoke, panting, her body soaked in sweat, the room hot and the orange lights still on, still tinting the room in fluctuations of amber. The lights felt alive. She had dreamt. What had she dreamt? Of her star, her lover.

Still alive. Searching her out.

A pain tugged at her, dug into her. She felt her mind splintering, breaking apart. He was dead. She had watched him die. She came as he went, the lights of galaxies filling her, embracing her. Exhaling her. Making her whole.

She laid her head back on the pillow, resisting the desire to call Mari. She was split between what she felt and what she knew. She could not see reality, not even in the middle, floating between the two like a bridge. Only illusions, faceted shadows, splintering into dizzying forms.

She could not go back to sleep.

She did not want to go back to sleep.

Instead she tossed and turned, trying to decide which had more reality, which had more gravity. Her dream and her intuition, or her memory?

XIII

The mozorro howled in wolfling pain, their lizard-skull faces shaking with each movement as they combed the ship, bursting with warning. The lights went from amber to a waxy red, the walls shaking and the bursts of hollow explosions ringing in their ears, trapped within the void of spaces.

Intruder! They howled, *Invader! Foreign!*

They called for the white blood cells to come storming through the ship with poison arms, wrapping and grasping the outsiders that walked amongst them. They sent warning chemicals to Itsasu, recorded images of the invaders for her to watch.

Itsasu stirred; the chemicals burned her skin.

The antibodies were withdrawn, their chemical compositions still forming. She would have to go as a doll and stop this herself. She only hoped her crew was prepared. This was war. This was suicide. They had no choice. Invaders could only be after one thing, the thing that Itsasu kept hidden in the secret part of the ship. The true meaning for her mission, the sole purpose of the last few centuries of her life.

The Ortzadar engine.

And there was no way she was going to give it up to some *pirates* storming her ship. No way she was going to just roll over and play along with their stupid little games. It would stretch her brain waves thin, but she commanded the computer to awaken four of her dolls and get them ready for war.

XIV

Mari ran to Ekhi's room, her boots sliding across the floor

as she came to an abrupt stop in front of the door, her heart on fire, her lungs struggling, her mind floating with a thousand thoughts. *Panic*, she thought. *Emergency*, she thought. In the distant echoes of the halls she heard the mozorro scream.

She forced the door open with a single thrust of her orange passkey. It slid aside reluctantly, the rust on the sides grating against the ceiling and sending a metallic dust below. In the circle of the doorframe, Mari saw a hollow-shelled room with the bed messed up and the blankets strewn across the floor in knotted piles. No sign of blood, no sign of struggle.

The butterflies in her skull cage leapt about, fluttering in fright. They spoke what Mari could not: danger, warning. Something in the ship. Something coming for them. Ekhi wasn't there, wasn't in her room. Mari hoped Ekhi was safe. Hoped Ekhi was someplace else, hiding in the secret corners of the ship.

She turned and let the door slide back to a close as the sound of footsteps penetrated her thoughts. The metallic clang-clanging of dolls as they stomped through the long, winding halls of the egia. She remembered when she was a child, living on one of the Norilian moons. She had gone swimming in the planet-sized lake, diving off the edge of the man-made island, the metal edges brushing her feet as she knifed into the water. Cold. Blue. Rushing around her.

And then she remembered seeing things, things on the bottom of the lake. She had known that her people had killed all of the original inhabitants, that the terraforming and the island had cost the natives their lives. But she had never seen it until that moment. Never seen that the bottom of the planet was one long graveyard, filled with the corpses of mermaids and mermen, their long hair whipping along with the waves, their eyes staring up in the leathery skull skin.

A fear. She had been afraid that they would reach up and grab her. That they would drown her to keep her down with them, forever on the bottom of the lake, swimming with them until she bubbled out of breath. Terraformed to death.

It was the same in the egia, this fear, this fear that these people could destroy them, could kill them. It came back fast, filling her every vein with that same panic she had felt as a child. Outsiders. Invaders. Those who wanted to kill her.

Crimson-faced war dolls stomped around the corner with ringing feet. All female, carrying betadurs in their hands, the rifle tips sparkling with gold and blue energy. Ready to fire. Ready to turn Mari into a pool of flesh and metal. They wore white aprons trimmed with red flowers, their waxy skin barely covered by the straps and fabric. They each had red hair that fell over faces and shoulders in wild, messy curls.

The dolls stopped when they saw her. Their feet stopped clang, clang, clanging; their marble eyes focused on Mari. "You are not him," one said, pointing the rifle at Mari, the tip glowing hot and the air tensing with magnetic spirals.

These were not Itsasu's dolls. Her dolls had an elegant grace, a sort of Neo-Victorian aesthetic. These were crude creatures. Sex puppets. War puppets. Something designed by a man, controlled by a man.

Mari looked at each of the dolls. "I'm not who?"

The mozorro screamed in the background.

"She is of no use to us. Continue the search."

They clanged past Mari, shoving her aside. The minute they were out of her sight she ran through the hallways, the honeycombed passages blurring past, her body in a panic, her mind filled with terror. With each moment, she remembered swimming down, seeing the graceful limbs dancing even in death. Her arms shook and her heart danced. But her mind, her mind was perfectly clear. Focused on a single goal: to be armed. To be ready.

She ran through the rec room and the half-filled mess hall, the mozorro screaming at her as she passed. She ran through bedrooms and entertainment parlors, and finally she ran to the docking station, the long hangar next to the main airlock.

The room was the largest in the egia, big enough for smaller ships to be docked inside of it. Above her head lay the ribs of the ship, gothic bone arches propping up the ceiling. At the far starboard end she saw that the air vent was open, and it led into a fragile glass tube suspended between two ships. A sucking sound came from the tube, like wet lips over a straw. She saw stars glitter beyond the tube, the walkway exposed to the infinite emptiness of the universe.

The light of a sun glittered off of the glass, reflecting a nearby planet and its trio of moons. The moons, they were blue and hovering, terraformed places, designed to keep human life. One was covered in water and gentle mechanical islands, and she thought again about the dead of her home planet and could not help but feel like she had come full circle in her life.

She walked calmly over to the line of lockers against the wall and pulled open her personal closet. She pulled out her suit, pulled out her own betadur. She slipped the black fabric over her head, hooking up the oxygen tubes, letting air flow through her suit. The cool artificial breeze tingled against her skin, giving her goose bumps and awakening some hidden cluster of memories nested in her mind. Memories of space. Of killing. She felt a change come over her, the suit clinging to her, masking her in its own memories.

This was a second skin. An exoskeleton. She felt insectoid, the memories of a hive mind crawling into her through the chitinous armor. Now she was the scavenger. Now she was the killer. This suit had seen death, had seen blood. It would see more, it would shed more. She twirled her betadur in her hands. It was heavy, hot. Enchanted. She felt the fire grow inside her.

And now, Mari thought, I beat them at their own game. They will see the thunder of my hands, feel the roaring waves of my heart burst upon them. They will tense and burn in my fire, their bodies crisp relics scattered across the stars.

As quietly as she could, she crept into the glass tube. She kept in the shadows, using the tricks of artificial light to hide her body as much as possible, letting the glow refract around her form and disguise it as shadows on the wall.

XV

Ekhi hid. She hid in the dark place, the unseen place. The place that was barely habitable. A tube that carried oxygen and hot air down through the vents below. She was curled in a ball, trying to close in on herself, one hand protectively grasping around the circle of her stomach.

It's them, she thought. The glass eaters. They'd come back for her even though the planet was gone, was burnt up, was nothing but asteroids now. That had to be them. They made the same loud clanging noise, had the same metallic voices.

She had thought she was safe. After so long, after so many years. How could she have thought that? Her brother's ghost still haunted her, and that meant they could, too. It meant they could hunt her and find her even though they should be dead. Because by all rights she should be dead too, dead over and over again. Because the world wyrms had eaten them all.

She crawled a little further into the vent, thinking. She tried to forget about the past, even for a moment. Tried to forget being twelve and hiding in the passages beneath the station, seeing the ground so far below and the moon so close above, fat and pregnant and full, just like now.

She tried to forget about them dragging Tobat's dead body through the tunnels. Tried to forget the trail of blood behind him. Like a snail. A red snail trail. A brother blood trail. The scraping sound of flesh on metal. She felt nauseated.

As a distraction from her memories, she decided to try to name her little girl. She knew it was a girl, no sensor or scanner necessary. A little girl whom she would keep safe. Keep alive and normal and brilliant. Naming her would be a way of moving out of the past and into the now. A chanting of names to calm and quiet her busy nerves.

Laino? Lurra? What was her name? Ekhi looked down at her stomach and asked in a whisper *What is your name, little girl? What is it?* Urtzi? Sorguin? Tronagarru? Maju?

None of the names fit. None of them felt right. The words entered her mind, whispered on the tingling tips of her lips, but died when spoken aloud. They were void words. Empty, meaningless words.

She heard a banging directly beneath her. And the sound of something sliding across the floor. And she knew, knew, knew it was her brother's body again. And again, and again. That body sliding, that wet red trail slicking the ground beneath him.

She leaned over. The air was so hot, so barely breathable. She was slick and sweaty and vomiting and nothing could keep her thoughts from smashing into one another, disrupting any coherence in her mind.

So she crawled and crawled and tried to make as little noise as possible. And kept trying on the shape of names, to see if they fit. Each word calmed her a little, while each sound beneath her took her back to that time, that time when Ekhi and her dad had climbed into the back of an egia and stole away aboard a ship to the skysea, leaving the wyrms to eat away at the glowing blue and gold world below and the glass eaters to tear her family to shreds, removing even their Patuek so there was nothing left of them to resurrect.

She heard a scraping sound beneath her, again. A hot thrust of air hit her, and Ekhi felt like her skin would burn right off and leave her ash and bone. She struggled and bit her tongue and climbed through the veins of the ship, the hot and sweaty veins, moving closer and closer into the heart of the egia.

That is where I will be safe, she thought. *The heart. It is safety.*

XVI

Hodei sat on his bed in the dark, hearing the chaos out in the honeycombs of the ship. He had his knife in his hands and his circular door closed, his clothes scattered in a messy pool on the floor.

I should get dressed, he thought. *I should go outside, grab a betadur and go fight.* Defend the ship. Save Ekhi. Show them what a hero he was, what a savior to mankind.

But he had a dread that swam around in his mind. A dread that he didn't quite grasp. In some way he knew that they were searching for him. Memories that were not his own bungled around in his mind, searching for shelf space. These memories danced under the surface of his own thoughts, tainting his fear. Birthday parties. Princess dresses. This was not his life, not his past. Yet there they were, taking up space in his mind.

This bothered him. So he cut into his arm. Single rings, not too deep. Enough so the memories of his own life that lay beneath the skin came bubbling up, with his blood, to the surface. *I am Hodei,* he thought. *I am Hodei.*

He crawled across the floor of his room, his fear still strong as it darted through his thoughts. And one thing came directly to him, one thought forced itself into his mental space: he must go and protect his magazines. There was something to this, something connected to those magazines that he could not quite understand.

His door slid open with the wail of scraping steel. He turned his head, his naked torso behind him, and saw the giant shadow of his brother. It cut the light into random shapes stacked onto one another. The gruff voice came out slow and final. Stone grating against stone. "Brother. Baby boy. I find you. No fairies. No healing. No saving. I hurt. I hurt."

A tool—a crowbar—sang in Sugoi's hand. An angry song, filled with violence.

Hodei was sick of this.He stood, naked. Like a Spartan. With each stab, with each leap and scream and bite and hit, he remembered the countless beatings, the countless times he had awakened in a bone-broken pain throughout his childhood.

Memory spun around him and through his mind like a thousand limbs, a thousand bodies. All motions echoed across time, rippling through mind and space, warping temporal reality. But the end did not change; the end never changed.

Smack. Crash. Crowbar to his face and him howling and bone-broken on the floor again, and the bar coming down, hitting, hurting. Soon he would be dead. Soon his skull would crack open and spill out his thoughts, his memories, stopping this endless abstract loop of limbs and violence. The only thing preserving his being, his memories, his thoughts, was his Patuek.

Sugoi's shadow. Angry. Covered in scarlet drops and bits of flesh. The crowbar glinting in the light of the hall-way. The sounds of wheels turning and brass spinning and gears singing and robotic limbs compressing and de-compressing. Clang, clang, clang. Metal feet on floors.

And before the bar could go down again Sugoi was on the floor, his head a messy splash of radiant light, his body a scarecrow skeleton, the architecture collapsing into a pile of unmoving limbs. Three war dolls stood in the hall, betadurs smoking, faces filled with mechanical glee.

Hodei was fuzzy. Drained. He recognized these dolls. Or rather, *she* recognized these dolls. Other memories tossing around in his head. The ports, the dream, the fly-ing and the materialization. Someone else was in him, not

just in his mind, but hidden in his genetic code, waiting to be awakened.

That girl, he thought.

The girl from the magazines.

The dolls motioned for him to come, to follow. And then—

One flew back against the wall, a mess of broken gears and melted wax and untangled wires without any purpose. The other two dolls turned around. More clang-clanging from the hall, more mozorro screams.

And Hodei.

Circles of shadow eclipsing the light.

He fumbles toward thought.

And ends up surrounded by dream.

And the spinning fractal lights of some beautiful girl's memories.

XVII

Itsasu saw through the eyes of her dolls, through the eyes of her mozorro, through the many-faceted eyes of the ship. She saw hundreds of images projected into the amber holofluid, saw them all and processed them.

The ship pumped adrenaline-laced chemicals into her body, reacting to her need for combat prowess and sharp, intense thinking. The dolls were in battle formation, her favorite battle dolls, weapons in hand, eyes staring ahead. Her gothic princesses, ready for war.

They would not take the Ortzadar engine from her. She

would destroy the ship first. It was far too important—she had spent centuries searching for it, keeping herself preserved through each archaic voyage from planet to planet, skipping amongst the stars like a pebble on a lake.

It was the key to bringing her husband back to life, the key to changing her whole existence for the better. And she had not spent the last 435 years being preserved in fluid, piloting this damn ship, for nothing.

She saw the foreign creatures standing in the hallway, red-haired war dolls. In secret, she sent one of her own dolls around through a different corridor, sneaking on board the intruders' ship while the other three dolls attacked. Combat ensued. Chemicals churned around her body, relating the war costs to her. Spiky tastes covered her tongue and shocks singed her body each time a war doll was hit and smoked and turned to a molten slab. Euphoric ambrosias of chemicals sang in her veins each time she blew one of the opposing dolls to slag.

She knew that the ship would need repairs. All this damage. All this damage was necessary. Dolls two and three blinked out. One left in combat, the other sneaking across the clear tube between ships.

She was not winning. Her combat doll was nearly dead. She smelled something like burning rubber, tasted foul dead things in her mouth as her body roared around her. Her skin roamed with the feeling of spiders underneath it.

The third doll crumpled to the ground. Right before the camera transmissions ceased, she saw Sugoi through the doorway, dead. Dead, dead. And maybe Hodei too. No mechanics to patch the ship. Fuck, she thought, fuck, fuck.

She set the mozorro over to watch the invading dolls, to see what they were doing while the heart of the ship churned out another handful of war dolls for her. It would be a moment or two for the assembly, but hopefully it would not be too late.

The mozorro eyes watched while sedatives coated her skin, making Itsasu sleepy and weary. She had to concentrate, to stay sharp, even though the ship wanted her to sleep, to rest. She saw the last war doll, battle-scarred and smoking, walk into the room and grab Hodei, lifting him up with mechanical arms and slinging him over its shoulder like he weighed nothing.

And then, in shock, Itsasu watched the doll storm off, clang, clang, clang, toward the exit. What strategy was this? Were they not after the Ortzadar engine? Had they come for Hodei all along?

She could not believe it.

XVIII

Mari walked unseen, the cameras blind to her, the servants that wandered the strangers' ship blind to her. She clung to the rust-coated walls, weapon pressed against her body, breathing slowly. In. Out. Oxygen trying to rush through her lungs, trying to burst through her veins in a fury of panic.

They can't see me, they can't see me. This became her mantra, her solace in this strange place. It was unlike any egia she had ever seen before—five times as large as Itsasu's ship.

The servants were strange as well. No mozorro on this ship, no dolls, no artificial constructs. No ship avatars either, just tiny elephant-headed humanoids with skin the color of fresh bruises. They wandered, fixing the ship, preparing food, not noticing her. Not seeing her. *Are these aliens,* Mari wondered, *or are they artificial beings, built for the purpose of keeping the ship in order?*

She wandered through the maze of the ship, the pathfalls unfamiliar. No sense of direction, no way of knowing where the mess hall was, the captain's quarters, the human crew. In fact, she noticed uneasily, there did not seem to be a human crew aboard this ship.

She had to be quick. The battery on the suit drained fast. Stealth mode ate away at the energy cells, and even the recharging nanofibers within the clothing could not bring in enough power to keep it going indefinitely. She hurried, controlling her footfalls. She did not want them to hear her empty steps and wonder if anyone was there, hiding.

Why are you here? she wondered. *"Why are you attacking us? What are you after?* She picked up the pace, the corridors empty as she further infiltrated the egia. The walls were circular, covered in rust and the sparkling light of silver webs that glued the interior of the ship together.

The captain's quarters must be around her some-where. Somewhere close by. She paused for a moment, looked around and saw nothing. Nobody in these hall-ways. Her breathing steadied, slowed even more. She pushed a lever on the side of her suit and felt light wash over her again, no longer an invisible girl. No longer in stealth mode.

She rolled on the tips of her toes, stretching herself out on the balls of her feet, feeling the betadur in her hands. She let the rifle cool, the coils unwrapping their charges, the weapon winding down, growing silent and dead.

I can rest here for a moment, plan ahead, she thought. *Figure out where I'm at, where I need to be.* She heard a ping, ping, pinging sound come from behind and turned around quickly enough to see a flash of light and then feel the hot sparking coils of a rifle blast burst through her shoulder blade.

She hit the floor and saw her attacker waddle up, smil-ing. One of those little purple ganeshas, carrying a cannon about five times its height. Smoking barrel. Little lips smil-ing behind twisted tusks.

She tried to move but could not. A cold numbness spread through her body. A paralysis, moving under her skin like a frost creeping through the forest of her nerves. Knees crumpled beneath her. Body glowing, dimming, shadow. She fell, her spine no longer supporting her, like a rag doll.

* * * *

XIX

Ekhi was in the beating heart, the trembling centersoul of the ship. She had fallen through rusted ductwork doors, moving past the spinning heat sensors, the blades of the great turbines churning in an ancient dance above her head.

She clanged on the metal floor, looked up at the circular rib ceiling, looked out the window at the vast sea of space, the infinite lights of stars sparkling in the distance. In front of her, the heart.

Trembling, beating. The heart of the ship. Big, bigger than she, four times her size, covered in cobweb-thin wires that crawled over it. Blinking lights, thinking lights. This was the motherbrain, the AI home of the ship.

Its ventricles pumped out commands into everything, controlled loosely by Itsasu in some chamber far away from the center. The red of its light coated everything. Ekhi was in awe. She had never seen an egia heart so close, so near to her. She reached out her hand, felt the muscle tense beneath her fingertips.

The memories of her past slipped away from her, the memories of her brother dying gone. She felt fire amongst her memories, sparking them, consuming them. She pulled her hand back, forcing herself to remember. *No, no,* she whispered to the heart. *I know you want to heal me. But I need those memories. The sorrow hurts, but that is what makes me human.*

She looked around the room, eyes tracing the manifold

wires connected to the giant beating muscle, wires laced with flickering lights communicating complex ideas and thoughts. A graphic display of AI complexity.

Next to the heart, discarded and dusty against the wall, was a human-sized blue egg-shaped tube. Inside of it she saw a face—old, male, standing upright. Eyes closed, hands clenched at his sides. Wrinkles covered his skin like a mess of folded fabric, his hair a clumpy shell of cloud dust. She walked over to him and examined the tube.

She thought he was dead, seeing large holes in his chest that led to a mummified cavity. She glanced at an LCD plaque that read the date of his imprisonment in flashing red and orange pixels. Almost eight hundred years ago. Far before the invention of the Patuek, and their ability to store a mind in stasis and be transplanted into a healed, cloned body.

Somebody loved you, Ekhi thought. *Somebody kept you here, with us. I only wish I could have done the same for my nova, my star, my love.* She remembered her dream. Was he still out there? No. No. He couldn't be.

Next to the tube was a small black box with a single orange jewel on top, flickering with a strange, dying light. This light gave off an amber glow and a silken milky mist that crawled across the top and dissipated, leaving an overpowering scent of apples.

"What are you?" Ekhi asked aloud, putting her hand against the side. Like the heart, it tensed. "What are you?"

XX

Hodei's head bobbed, the mechanical shoulder bruising his ribs, coiled wiry hair brushing harshly against his face. He looked above, tilting his head back, seeing first the ribs of a ship, then iron ducts coated in rust, then bones, then glass above him letting in the light of stars and three blue moons. He didn't know why they wanted him, what they could ever want to do with him.

His whole body was bruised, tattered, bones smashed by his idiot brother. Fuck, Hodei thought, he's dead now. The thought stung his mind more than his nerves stung with pain, raising up a curious series of emotions that raced around in his mind.

He would've killed me. Yet, he's my brother. Now Mari is free, and he definitely can't pursue Ekhi now. Yet, he's my brother.

Other thoughts bubbled up under his skin, hot blooded thoughts, thoughts of *her*, that magazine girl. The ship above him—the webs of electrical light that coated it, the strange bruise-colored elephants that swept and cleaned—this was her brother's ship.

The last time she had been on it was over forty years ago. At least, that was her last memory, when they were around the moons of Titan, still within the solar system of Manhome itself. They had been planning to visit the Oort cloud next, maybe fly down and start a farm on one of the terraformed planets that ringed around the light of a blinking red sun.

Her brother's wife had died about a week before this memory. Hodei felt the magazine girl's sadness; the two had been best friends. She had even been the maid of honor at her brother's wedding. The death had come as a sudden shock to both of them, and she felt such sadness not only for her brother, but for herself.

Her sister-in-law had died quickly, her mind attacked by a linguistic virus known as the sakre. It destroyed her Patuek and turned her brain into a puddle of milk in her skull.

The magazine girl had never asked to see the vidding of the incident. She knew of the damage, had witnessed it as a nurse a few years before when she had been an intern on some dust speck of an asteroid floating through the outer rim of the Milky Way. Her brother had told her about the whole thing, the words far worse than any visual recording. He had tried to stop the spread of the virus, tried to save her Patuek.

He was too late—he awoke to her body shaking, her body screaming, her body vibrating, eyes rolling around, teeth bursting through gums. He told his sister that he remembered reaching over and holding his wife down, pinning her wrists with his fists, screaming for the ship AI to send in help. For anyone to come and help them.

By the time help came, white milk had leaked out of her ears and pooled around her head. Her mind was gone, her Patuek, gone. Nothing to revive. He kept her body around, even though the magazine girl had insisted on disposing of it, burning it, getting rid of the sakre that might still be waiting to whisper itself on the corpse's lips, infecting them all.

Hodei pushed these memories back, away from his mind. He was crying; he couldn't help himself. She had infected him with her thoughts, with her emotions, and it felt so vaguely alien, so strangely unreal. As if his existence until this moment had been a dream and she was his true thought, his true mind, his true master.

XXI

Itsasu pushed past the numbness, the floating dreaminess that engulfed her body in her liquid prison. She flapped her arms, called the computers of the ship to come and aid her. *Be my eyes, be my eyes,* she sang out. She felt fluid beat out from her cage, singing through the ship, carrying chemical messages to the beating heart of the egia.

I need to know, she whispered. *Damages. Tally up the damages.* She looked through the floating dust camera eyes, through mozorro eyes, through a thousand eyes, seeing all the things that had been damaged. Holes blasted, walls melted, yet nothing too terrible. Nothing that couldn't be fixed within an hour or so.

The heart of the ship then spoke to her, its voice ancient, filled with a sentience from before her time. She had not heard the ship speak in over a decade, and the sound of it placed fear into her frail paper heart.

This ship can destroy us with a single whisper. I am talking to it right now, intellect to intellect, using our ancient ways of radiospeak. They mean us no harm. They will un-dock from us when an experiment is finished. If we dis-connect or move, or try to send anyone on board to res-cue Hodei, the ship will sing to us in a chorus of flames, and we will be destroyed in such a way that none will be revived.

Itsasu swam, letting her thoughts roll around in her head, buoyant. *Do they know of what we keep?*

A silence. She felt a smile, somehow, hung in her mind. A mental pulling back of lips, of cheek, of teeth grit-ting together. *No,* the ship said, *but someone else does. Our little stowaway. Although she knows naught of what she sees.*

Itsasu blew with weak lips at the holographs of the damage to the ship, scattering them in a whispering wisp of firefly light. She muttered a curse under her breath. *She'll have questions, questions I do not want to answer.*

The heart of the ship took form as an avatar in her fluid: red skin, horned head, shadowy black cloak torn and tattered behind it, skull-faced and shadowed. *Never mind her. Sugoi is dead. You should at least back up his Patuek, if not heal him.*

Itsasu clenched her body tightly, her nerves and frail muscles like a fist. She felt skin cracking into dust, float-ing away in a clay mist. *That fool, why should I heal him? He almost killed his brother. We don't need that kind of friction on the ship.*

The AI's flickering flame of a figure began to melt away into the holofluid. *Erase some of his mind, then. Not all of it—whatever memory made him want to kill his brother. That should snuff out the Cain instinct for now.*

Itsasu called up the holos for the section of the ship Sugoi was in. She saw the mess of his body and felt a strange detached pity. She wanted to leave him dead. He was far worse a man than her husband. Why did this stupid fool deserve life?

I'm waiting, Itsasu. Bring him back. Or I cut off your lifeline, leaving you to drift on in death, waiting for someone to revive you. How would you like that? Who would save your husband then?

Itsasu floated through the fluid, her teeth grinding together, brittle, frail things. *Damnit, okay. I'll bring him back. But fuck taking out that memory. That's too much work, and we have too much to do. But if he attacks his brother one more time, I'm leaving him to die in the endless vacuum.*

There was no response, just an empty humming in the darkness. The heart of the egia had left her. Its ghost was gone, expelled into the shadows of the ship once again.

Fuck, she thought as she called the thalna to Sugoi's body, *you don't deserve this. You don't deserve what I'm about to do.*

XXII

Mari still couldn't move. The numbness was gone and it left a fine prickly feeling along her spine. Webbing stretched across her body, heavy silver that bound her tight, leaving only her face visible in the stark darkness of the ship.

She felt drained, like her blood had seeped out of her body and left her an empty husk. She wondered briefly if Sugoi was all right, if the ship was still there. She might be the last living person from Itsasu's crew. The whole ship might be just scattered star ash by now.

She turned her head, barely, the webbing weighing her neck like stones; a sound came from down the hallway where the light flickered green and white and the ceiling dripped a rusted red fluid with a harsh echo. The sound of machinery, of clockwork, of banging metallic doors and the whirring of ancient steel sentience.

A doll walked up to her, a pretty, petite thing wearing a red flowered dress and coiled red hair. The eyes were not orbs, but instead flashlights, letting out hot white halos from LED eyes. The jaw dropped down, a nutcracker jaw with a tiny speaker inside, not even feigning speech. The voice was distorted, mechanical, reproduced. Not human.

"Our scan shows two things. One, you are not infected. Two, you are not carrying the Patuek."

Mari tried pushing her limbs out, straining her body against the webbing. She was stuck. "Okay. Good. Great. What the fuck does that mean?"

"It means that you are useless to us, and will be discarded of properly."

Mari laughed. It was a hard, bitter sound. A laughter that rolled around on her tongue, leaving the taste of tin in her mouth. "Great. Just great."

The doll stomped away from the room and Mari wondered if Sugoi would come and burst down the walls, tearing the ship apart to save her. She wondered if Itsasu would bring her dolls in, betadurs blazing. I can't die here, she thought, not now. Not in this webbing. This is a mistake.

She pushed her limbs against the webbing, felt her muscles shove against the steel membrane. It felt as if it were going to give, to break, to snap. And then nothing. It still held her down, still tense, still captive in its strong arms.

She sobbed, briefly, fearing death; her tears dripped down her cheeks and then caught in the webs that contained her. Not even those had release, had freedom. Trapped, trapped. Until they disposed of her.

XXIII

Ekhi sat in the heart of the ship, staring at its beating red and veiny skin, listening to it talk with each beat of blood flowing through it. The room was hot and the air tasted salty, like she was caught in the bloodstream of a giant. The heart did not project an avatar of itself into a holofield when it talked to her, nor did it use a doll or a replicant. It just spoke, the voice riding through the air in a sweaty fever dream.

I have had many captains pilot me, many men and women drive me through the starsea. I have seen more worlds than any human, seen more deaths in my lifetime than I could care to see. I was a research vessel. That was my first mission, and, it seems, my only mission. My eternal mission. My original creator died, his work unfinished. Even through all these centuries I have not seen anything like it.

Ekhi walked up to the box, staring at it, trying to peer into it, see if she could open it somehow. Sealed shut on all sides. And the jewel on top of it seemed to be a part of the box, not cut into the shape, but instead a natural extension of it.

"Anything like what?" she asked.

She had been in the heart of the ship for a few hours, talking with the AI off and on throughout that time, waiting until she felt it was safe to go back outside. She trusted the heart of the ship, felt like the heart and the AI where the only things aboard this vessel she could believe were telling her the truth. It was the only person she had met so far without motive. Without a need to betray her or anyone else.

She didn't feel vulnerable when she was around it. She felt strong, trustworthy.

Well, it responded in its ancient voice, *like this other ship that has attacked us and kidnapped Hodei. When I spoke to it, the onboard AI didn't feel right. It felt panicked. It sounded obsessed. I can't explain it. Like a human, it sounded love-torn and hungry.*

Ekhi felt her stomach, felt the worlds explode and expand, the new galaxy growing by each moment, each second. She noticed that her stomach was distending a little.

Not much, just a little. A hard little bump, like a rock had slid under her belly skin.

"Maybe it's not an AI," she said. "Maybe it's piloted by humans entirely. I've heard of some ships doing that. Especially really old ones, when the AI had broken down, unwound. Gone insane."

She paused for a moment, and then said in a whisper, "My ship was like that. Before. Before I came here. I needed to shut it down. Pilot it in the nude, without a heart of any help. It was sad, the moment I told that AI to sleep. It still hurts me to think about it."

The heart beat faster for a moment, the ventricles straining, plumping, almost bursting. She walked away, slowly, thinking that it might explode and shower her with whatever juice powered this ship.

I'm sorry, it said. *I've heard that piloting an egia can be very stressful for a human. It can take a large toll on the mind.*

Ekhi shrugged, picked up the box. It was cold to the touch—too cold. Her fingers burned from the cold, the feeling running through her skin like ice in her blood. She dropped it, watching it fall slowly and gracefully like a feather, and then dipped her fingers into her mouth, trying to warm them with her tongue.

"I know. It did, I think. Some of my memories, where I held the controls of the ship in my mind, they're missing. Like holes in my being, ripping through all levels of thought. I feel partial somehow, broken, because of it. But I couldn't stop, I needed to see my lover. We were to be married, did you know that? Married. But he died."

The ship's heart slowed down, paused. Thump, thump, thump. Ekhi sat down on the floor, her hand over the bump in her stomach, feeling the ghost of stars swim beneath her skin.

I'm sorry. What happened to the ship's heart?

Ekhi closed her eyes, the holes in her mind swimming around in her thoughts. She remembered this—yes, she remembered this clearly. It had been backed up by her Patuek, stored in its memory chambers so that she would never forget it, no matter how hard she tried.

"It went insane," she said. "The programs broke down. Entropic. I'm not sure how it happened, or why. If I could've gotten to a port in time, they could've fixed it. Scanned the heart and removed whatever it was that ate the algorithms, making it act in such a cruel way. But I couldn't stop, don't you see? I had to go see my lover. And I'm glad I did. If I would've been even moments later, he would have gone nova without me. And then what would I have? Not even his memory, not even his daughter. It was worth it."

Silence was the response. Ekhi walked over to the door, put her hand against the rusted circular frame and tried to feel if there was still danger, if the ship was still under attack.

A sigh. *It's a pity your ship had to die for your love. It's safe outside, if you want to go now. Although be careful, the life form readings from inside the ship that had attacked us are, well, peculiar. They have some genetic servants aboard, but that's not exactly what I'm picking up. Something foreign.*

Ekhi raised an eyebrow. "Do you mean an alien?"

No response. She laughed, her pregnant stomach rocking against her ribs with each hearty ha-ha-ha. She stopped for a moment, wiped tears from her cheeks, caught her breath. "Are you serious? Almost every sentient alien life form that we have met has been obliterated by coming into contact with us. So what, is there a new breed of alien that we haven't met, hiding in the cosmos? Or is this something else?"

The AI paused, choosing its words carefully. *Close. I don't know. It's not like anything I've seen before. It's alien, but it's in a human. Maybe a human changed? Genetically? I have no idea. I can't tell from this distance. My scans are inaccurate.*

The door beside her slid open automatically with a screech and wail of rust freshly disturbed. She walked out, her bare feet warm against the cold metallic cage of the floor.

Yes, that's it, the ship said, *changed humans. At least, that's part of it.*

XXIV

Hodei was on the floor, his body thrown down into a chaotic mess of limbs and shattered bones. His whole skin ached, his nerves bursting into radial rings of pain. He mewled on the floor, a pathetic noise.

Against the wall at his head were two large cylinders filled with an icy blue liquid. The cylinders were decorated with intricately complex vine motifs, crawling over the edges and down the sides like a living thing carved out of gold. The leaves folded over, each spot and vein accurately represented in a perfect replication of real vegetation. Suspended in the cylinders were two human bodies, one male and one female, their hair messy tendrils waving through the fluid.

Hodei recognized them and felt his heart tighten, the muscles tensing like a fist. That was her, the girl from the magazine, and him, her brother. Over their mouths were insectile breathing masks, like scorpions wrapped around their jaws. They were in suspended animation of some sort. Hodei had never seen technology like this. In the fluid danced the flickering firefly lights of the thalna, stitching the bodies back together with each second, keeping them in a constant state of health and well-being.

He reached his hand out, painfully, his fingers twisted into a broken claw shape, touching the edge of her cylinder. The glass slid beneath his fingers, making a squeaking sound.

A small doll sat next to him, watching him with big black button eyes and fabric lips, sewn fingers and stitched teeth. Its hair was made from curling yarn. This was not one of the dolls who had brought him on the ship, those waxy almost-human manikins. No, this was a child's toy brought to life with complex nanomachineries crawling beneath the fabric, running close to the cotton like computerized weevils.

It spoke from a tiny black speaker stitched into its mouth, sticking out like the eyes of an insect. "It has taken me so long to find you, to scan you and see that she is inside of you, her Patuek. When I became infected—when the heart of the ship even became infected—I had to take such drastic measures. To slow down the sakre before it destroyed us all."

Hodei twitched a little, convulsing uncontrollably. Everything was painful. Breathing. Talking. Moving. Everything.

"It was horrible, horrible, happening so fast. I had to hide her Patuek before they, too, became infected. I shot them through space, riding the radio waves and coming into your body. I was able to slow it enough in myself, before my Patuek were eaten by the sakre. The heart of the ship and the crew were not so lucky."

Hodei felt his blood vibrate and he remembered, remembered her name, he knew it now. Iuski. It whispered to him in his blood, sang her name through his veins. The name lit up his mind, lit up his memories, brought her personality out so fast that it flooded everything inside of him with glowing halos of her own thought, her own Patuek searching for meat to latch onto, meat to be reborn with.

She remembered, inside of his skin, under his thoughts. She remembered hearing that word, that foul and tainted alien word. Her mind was invaded—other thoughts, foreign thoughts, taking over, thinking for her, being her. Memories of an alien landscape, of a world full of ruined cities and a burnt-out shell of a sun. Her thoughts were translated into another tongue, some alien language she had not heard before, these new words changing her own thoughts, her own memories. Trying to rewrite her. Trying to transform her in their puppet.

I don't want to remember this, Hodei thought, pushing it aside. She can remember that. When she is in her own body.

He looked up at her body, a perfectly preserved sack of meat without soul, mind or memory. Her naked body was holy in person, no longer something made from glossy pages and airbrushed into perfection, but instead a flawed, angelic figure floating in a blue prison, her moles and scars making her more beautiful than he could ever have believed possible.

Staring at her, she saw herself through his eyes and became her own object, objectified through the male gaze, and then became herself. She remembered the first time she had taken that job, posing as a model on some port hung outside of a low-burning blue sun. Her first series of nude images, how uncomfortable she felt, smiling for the camera. How cold it was, without clothing.

And then later looking at the end result, the magazine, remembering what it felt like to see herself like that, as an object of sexual desire reflected on the page. It was unreal; that could not have been her. Could not ever be her. That woman on the pages was someone else, trapped on the glossy pages. Someone that looked like her from a distance, like a hidden twin, shoved in the background of her life.

Hodei forced the memories out again, feeling sick inside his stomach. This was wrong. Seeing her thoughts, reflecting his thoughts, it made her less perfect, debased her in his mind. He did not want to converse with her, did not want to understand her. "Take her out of me," he said to the doll. "Take her out of me. Please."

The doll walked up to him, put a sewn hand against his face. It felt like a washcloth, brushing against his cheek. And her remembered his mother, so long ago, washing his face in a sink on a newly terraformed moon hung over the red skull of a wasted Earth.

"I can't. Not yet. I might even put my own Patuek into you, for the time being. Have you carry us back to your ship. You are not infected. We are, still. I've slowed it down, but if we are released now, all will be lost. We would be dead before long, and then you would catch it, too. We would whisper the word once, just once, and your mind would become a slave to this foreign tongue, this alien thought device."

Hodei tried to move away from the doll's stubby white paw, tried to push his cheek back and out its washcloth caress. Too much pain. Too much. He could only flinch slightly, and then moan.

"First, we need to fix you up. You will be useless to us if you stay a broken shell. Then you will bring our bodies aboard your ship with you."

Hodei felt something like cotton being wrapped across his skin, mummifying him in its gauzy substance. "What if I say no?"

The doll smiled a sewn grin, black button eyes shining. "Too late," it whispered. "The process has already begun."

XXV

Sugoi's body was on fire. His head was a mess of bees and ants and screaming things. His mouth was open, toothless, being put back together atom by atom, his whole being erupting in a wall of broken glass, shattering across his nerves in a wave of blinding pain. He pushed himself up on his hands, twisted, bent, being bent backwards, bending back, firefly lights forcing his body the correct way, fixing bones, forcing things back to normal.

He howled and wailed as bone stitched back and brain stitched back and body stitched back. Face bursting, blood, pain, then put back together again, the thalna taking him apart and sewing him into a living thing, their tiny computational matrices rebuilding him from the ground up.

When they were done, he sat arm in hand, his mind hollow and jellied. He had nothing. No idea. Then his Patuek came out, came out in tiny fingers, pried open the grey lines of his brain, dug their memories down under the flaps of brain matter, placed the thoughts from before back into his skin.

The dolls. The brain bust. *Hodei touched her.*

Sugoi smiled. He stood up, his body moving thickly, slowly, the thalna fluttering off now that their work was done, their tiny engines sounding like the whispering of hummingbird wings. The mozorro crawled away from him, and through the intercom he heard the voice of Itsasu, scolding him.

She went on and on, berating him for hurting his brother, her words buzzing around in his thoughts but leaving no impact. He ignored her words, her reprimands, and instead focused on the fire that grew inside of him, focused on his hate.

"Now, before we get back to work on fixing this ship, I need you to get Hodei and Mari back, and then to disengage with our attacker. We'll use what we can and hit the entanglement engine, moving far away from their ship and leaving no trail behind us for them to follow."

Sugoi cracked his neck, his arms, his newly built bones. Fire burst inside of his chest, a red giant of a sun dancing beneath his ribs. *Oh,* he smiled, *oh.* He would go and get them. But rescuing, that was not part of it. He had his own plans. To hell with Itsasu.

He ran over to the docking station, where he knew the other ship had connected with theirs. The ribs of the ship dashed over his head like some alien language imprinted on the world. His body still hurt, but now it was an aching burn.

He kicked open his locker, his giant form shadowing the room like a sinister creature. He pulled out his betadur and his numen suit, strapping them on, charging the hot coils of the rifle. He smiled. He could not help it, even though it hurt his mouth, like a scalpel against his cheeks. He smiled.

The sucking of the tube called to him, sang to him. A siren song of flowing air, the glass suspension between the ships reflected the city lights of the moons and the glittering dust of the stars.

Hodei and Mari would both pay. They couldn't do that to him, to Sugoi. Couldn't leave him for dead. Couldn't have those dolls kill him. No. He would smash them both. They had done it on purpose, cheated on him and hired some thing to come and kill him. But he would show them. He had the upper hand now.

His own brother. His girlfriend. Had the last four years meant nothing? Had the lifetime of keeping his baby brother safe meant anything? They left him for dead. Assassinated, while they ran off to fuck on some docked ship. Probably going to leave without him, leave him behind with that mummified Itsasu and that weird pregnant girl.

Not going to happen, he thought. *They all die now.*

XXVI

Mari tried to move. Something was coming, blasting, burning; was it coming for her? To save her or to kill her? The webbing was too strong, steel strong, keeping her bound and wrapped up.

Stomping feet and a hollering howling sound—Sugoi's animalistic, angry, no-longer-man voice. A caged creature voice, released and burning and destroying, a hungry, howling, eating voice. Bursts of sound, ringing around in her head—betadur bursts, metallic clanging of things hitting the ground—and a smell of sweet fire and steel igniting and smelting.

Mari wondered if he was here to save her. That wasn't a happy sound, it was a violent, terrible sound. She remembered threats he had made to her, always in the middle of the night, his back outlined by the harsh light of space, his features a wall of shadows. "I could kill you," he would say, waking her from sleep, "I could kill you. Please don't make me do it."

She let it slide because he never laid a hand on her, and she had always thought he was bluffing. But now, with this raging anger, this howling voice, she wondered. Was he here to murder her as he had always promised?

She held her breath, quick, quiet, in her lungs, trying to keep it hidden beneath her ribs. Heart goes thump, thump, arms struggle. Too hard. Not enough freedom.

His shadow bent out—she saw it, like a hundred arms, limbs twisted, a mountain of man, craggy and ancient. She saw him walk into the room, his numen suit glowing a strange mixture of gold and blue, a hundred doll parts around his body like war trophies. In his hand a glowing betadur, the chambers hot and ready to spark.

His face was twisted, molten rock, bursting forth, his eyes hatred volcanoes. He pointed the gun right at her. Her eyes closed, she whimpered. "Please," she pleaded, "please, no."

He stormed forward, pointing the rifle at her, waving it at her like an expression of himself, an extension of his anger. "You hurt. Why? Why hurt me? Huh?"

"Sugoi," she said, her eyes still closed, her voice trembling, trying to stay calm, cool. "I don't know what I did to hurt you. I'm so sorry, okay? But I didn't do it on purpose. I need you to help me get down. Before they kill me here."

She heard the betadur blast, a harrowing Tesla coil sound, saw crackling of lightning and then felt the steel webbing melt from around her. For a second she thought she was going to die, that the bolt would blast through her heart, ripping it to shreds, and then Itsasu would have to revive her. Somehow.

Instead her body hit the floor. Her lungs expanded, no longer caught tight by the webbing. She felt the steel floor of the ship beneath her hands, and just about kissed the ground. She looked up at Sugoi, saw his face in torment and torture, his eyes flaring, his lips twitching.

"I free. See? Not bad guy. Not bad. Why? Why you leave? For dead? Why Hodei touch you?"

She stood up, hugged him, brought his giant body close to hers. She felt him beneath the numen suit, his skin distant and packed beneath the layers of fibers and metal. She held him close, even though he tried to pull away. "I don't know why. Okay? He was trying to comfort Ekhi. It has nothing to do with us."

He pushed her away, teeth clenched together like iron bars across his face. "Yes. It does. He touch. I hurt. I love you. So, you go. Go."

She turned and ran, back the way she had come. She stumbled and swerved, her feet still filled with tiny prickles, her body trying to lose the stumbling numbness. Her numen suit clanged as she walked. She had originally come over to stop the invasion on the ship, but now knew that Sugoi would probably end up destroying them all. She had to go back to Itsasu, warn her of this.

Mari only hoped that the two ships were still connected somehow, that she had enough time to go back and stop Sugoi from killing Hodei. She only hoped Hodei had stayed on that ship, had not tried to do something stupid and heroic that would get them all killed.

XXVII

Hodei lay flat as the Patuek entered under his fingernails, through his tear ducts, his ears, mouth and nose, slicing under his skin like tiny razors, peeling back his mind and storing themselves beneath his blood. He howled and punched the metal floors, the sound ringing around him like a metallic giant walking.

They cut up his memories, cut into his mental architecture, burned holes into his thought patterns. He was to be the host for their escape, a last sanctuary of their minds before the disease destroyed them.

The doll leaned up, looked at him, smiling. "I'll accompany you onto the ship. Help you slide the bodies on board."

Hodei bit the inside of his cheek, his teeth grating against the flesh. "Itsasu will notice. Will see us come in."

"I've already notified your ship's AI of our plans and

needs. It will keep Itsasu in the dark. It seems to think she would not understand our situation. Don't worry, it has us covered."

Hodei thought back to the first time he had met the heart of the ship, back when he had joined Itsasu's crew and took a tour of the egia. He did not like the strange mind, its bellowing voice, its bizarre wisdom culled from centuries of intelligence algorithms evolving and learning and storing information into complex data matrices. The very existence of the heart of the ship gave him an odd feeling, like the ship was haunted by some dead god peering into their lives.

Hodei stood up, painfully, glancing at the two tubes. "You want me to drag those into our ship? In a way no one will notice?"

The doll nodded proudly. "Correct," it said.

Hodei leaned against a wall, propping up his aching spine. His body felt new and barely healed, as if he had grown in a vat and then been released into the wild. Each limb ached from the thalna's reconstruction and the invasion of the Patuek. "Why do you need me? Need us? You can travel the void of space on your own until you find a way of stopping this, can't you? Reversing it somehow?"

The doll's black button eyes shimmered unnaturally, tiny cameras nested inside them, taking everything in, recording it and storing the information for later. "There is something on your ship. You will see. Just do this for us, and you will be paid very well."

Hodei shrugged. He wasn't looking forward to lugging

the two tubes through the ships. If only there were a way to turn the artificial gravity off while he did it. But people would notice that, would get suspicious. And if that happened, these invaders could turn his insides into a pulp within minutes and then find a new host.

The door slammed open behind him, an abrupt movement that knocked him to the floor. He sprawled, his back vulnerable once again. The shadow of the body in the doorway was a giant, staring down at him. A craggy old thing, earthy smelling and full of rage.

His brother. Sugoi.

Sugoi held the betadur, his eyes filled with murder, his teeth rigid in his mouth, keeping his tongue inside. He leapt forward, weapon in the air as the doll stared on in terror. "I Kill!" Sugoi screamed. "I kill. Brother baby no more. No more. I kill."

The weapon was slung forward and pointed at Hodei's eyes. He watched as his brother's finger tickled the trigger; the coils lit up, the segments bursting with culminations of powerful energy. Then--then, abruptly, the hand was flung back, screaming, shaking, the weapon flopping to the ground and scattering across the floor. The giant was in pain, his hair smoking as if it were on fire, his eyes bulging out of his head, his knees on the ground, his fists pounding against his cheeks, his nails digging beneath the skin.

Hodei scrambled back, his spine against the glowing blue cylinders. They were cold against his back, freezing to the touch, almost burning his skin. He watched his

75

brother flail about for a few minutes more, sparks running along Sugoi's body, his face twisting and fingers yanking the skin away from the muscle. The screams ate into Hodei's mind. Sugoi had come to kill him, yet he still felt pity and fear for his brother.

Eventually the screams stopped and the body slumped over with a xylophone sound. Hodei leaned forward, unsure if it was safe to move. He kicked the body with the tip of his toes. Sugoi made no response.

The doll looked up at him. "Now is the time to go. His life readings show that he is still alive, just not in his body."

Hodei sighed, not wanting to go through with this, but seeing no other way out. He reached behind and grabbed the cold cylinder. The thing practically weighed nothing at all. He slung it over his back and proceeded to walk out the door, tiptoeing over his brother's body. He would come back for Iuski next, and only hoped that his brother would not be awake before then. He stopped in the doorway for a moment, looking over her beautiful body again.

She saw him look at her, saw the way his eyes moved over her body. It brought back more memories. The first time she made love, it was in a low orbit cruiser above some lost and ruinous planet. The first boy she had kissed, not even ten years old, in an alleyway behind her house.

Hodei shoved these thoughts beneath his own complex thoughts, hiding them beneath his own intricate memories. As he did so, her brother's thoughts bubbled up. *Don't push us down, don't push us away. Doing so kills our Patuek, kills that memory. Do that and you will exterminate us, wipe us out completely.*

Hodei smiled. That might not be a bad thing.

It would wipe her out, too, the brother thought, *and I know you love her. Or at least you think you do. I'm thinking that's not something that's on your agenda, killing the girl you're infatuated with.*

Hodei cursed and moved out of the doorway and into the skeleton of the hall, the ceiling above him lined with flickering songs and the eyes of tiny mechanical creatures. The doll crouched on the lightweight canister, hitching a ride as Hodei walked.

"So who was that? Who just tried to kill us? Your brother?"

Hodei grunted. "Don't want to talk about it. Let's keep going."

The doll climbed up the canister, the blue light from inside tainting the doll's patchwork skin. "You know, if he kills her before we get back, she's going to need a body. Your body, probably."

Hodei said nothing. He just kept walking, lugging the canister over his shoulder, trying not to think, not to succumb to the echoing thoughts and memories of brother and sister that raced around in his mind, crawling beneath his memories, tainting and overwriting him.

XVIII

"He won't be able to kill his brother."

The words danced out of the mouth of a newly built doll, standing with a melty wax face in a long, winding corridor. The eyes were still half-finished globes, oozing and blinking with red and orange LEDs. The teeth were yellow and cloudy, and beneath the skin Mari saw the flickering scales of gold and orange fish swimming, creating Itsasu's new doll from their electronic excretions.

Mari's butterfly twitched about in her steel skull, doing a fevered dance that was close to mania. It reflected her own disbelief, and her own inner turmoil. "Why not?" Mari said, exasperated.

"Because I snipped his nerves and attached a small black beetle to the knotted, combined ends of them. This birao is enriched with his brother's genetic code. If it senses that he will try to hurt the person with that DNA, it attacks his nervous system, immobilizing him. Brutal, but much easier than the alternative the ship's heart suggested."

Mari's stomach burned and twisted. She resisted the urge to vomit, held it inside of her, thrusting the feeling down into the background of her thoughts. "That's—that's inhumane. How could you do that to him? What right have you to do that to him?"

The doll's half-made lids blinked, almost closing over the melting, goopy eyes. The shutters of the lids looked like camera irises from years gone by. "He was dead. The invaders had blown his head into a mess upon the floor. I did not want to revive him. Rather, I would have stored his Patuek in a database, and then maybe used his skills in an android of some sort. Something I could easily control and keep in check. But the ship's heart wouldn't have it."

A pause. Mari held in a wave of emotion that threatened to take over her body. Nausea erupted into violence and hatred like a volcano of sickness inside her. "You would take him away from me?"

"It doesn't matter, either way. He's alive now. I have no idea why the ship's heart insisted on it. But he is alive now. If you'll excuse me, I need to finish this doll and start repairs on the ship. Hodei has a lot of work to do when he gets back, as does his brother."

The doll walked away, its mechanical feet leaving a slurry of nanoparticles across the floor, a disgusting wet sludge of silver and metal. "And you have a lot of work to do as well. We're going to use the entanglement engine once we have everyone back on board. It seems the threat has been minimized. We'll close off the tube they used to invade and then burst out of here in a ray of light. I need you to calculate a solar path of least resistance."

Mari nodded. The anger was gone, the violence, the nausea. When her mind entered navigator mode it was all work. A role that she had spent her life perfecting. "I'll have it to you within a few minutes. What is our destination?"

"The Aatxe Port. If rumor is correct, a shop of relics there has the last piece I need. Then we can all go our separate ways and leave space to those who wish to travel it. Won't it be nice? To have this finally done, no longer a nomad amongst the stars."

Mari sighed and walked back toward the navigation chambers. "Okay, I'll get right on it."

She did not want this to end, did not want to go to some planet and settle down. Sugoi, she knew, would probably take off the moment this trip was done. And where would that leave her? Sure, Itsasu paid well, but if the voyage was over, then she would be rich and lonesome. And she couldn't have that. She needed him nearby. She counted on his giant presence, his oversized hands, his earthy smell. Counted on it to always be there with her. If his presence became a void, then her loneliness would swallow her whole.

XXIV

Sugoi rolled over. His whole body stung and smelled of burnt skin and rubber. His limbs were hot and sore, his mind numbly searching for thoughts through the pain. He had dreamt for a moment there, dreamt of flying around a large planet that fired missiles at him, burning holes into his skin. When he awoke he was alone in the room. Even those weird canisters that his brother had were gone.

He sat up, looking around, trying to see if there was any sign of life. "Lo?" he called out. "Lo? Anyone?"

No answer. He slid upright, and then realized with a panic that he was on a foreign ship and was hunting Hodei, and that when he had tried to kill Hodei, he had felt pain. The memory of pain stung at him, tasting him with the poison of its recollections.

He stood and moved toward the direction from which he had come, remembering the ship in a vague blur of running. *Hodei go this way*, he thought. *Must track. Must kill. Venge, venge, venge.*

He pushed through the walls, his numen suit like a parasite wrapped tightly around his body, almost suffocating his pores. He tried to remember the way he had come, the way back to the ship, tracking Hodei. Killing Hodei was the main thought on his mind. His brother had stepped too far. He must be corrected.

He heard a whispering sound from behind, like a knife cutting through fabric. He turned and saw a small humanoid elephant, probably a servant, genetically altered and built for space travel. It had purple skin that made Sugoi think of the first time had he punched his brother, the color of the bruise that had risen against the brown flesh. It made him smile.

"What you want, little thing? Eh?"

The elephant creature smiled, pulled up its trunk to reveal tiny human lips surrounded by tusks. It spoke, whispering quietly, just loudly enough for Sugoi to hear. "Shazarttta tatta tat haratta," it said, its voice like a rapid-fire machine gun. "Shazarttta tatta tat haratta."

The words were a sequence, Sugoi realized, a pattern. His mind tried to unravel the pattern, tried peeling apart its complex structure. In revenge the word pattern folded in on itself, covering up his memories, unlocking parts of his mind with violent jigsaw fingers. New words sprang up, removing old words from his mental landscape, replacing the symmetry of his slow thoughts with new symbols, new language, his own mind invaded by an alien tongue forcing itself into his thoughts, raping his consciousness. His old memories were replaced with communal memories in this new language, memories on a distant planet with four moons and a bright orange star that shouted out all shadows and covered the horizon in an orange light.

And he remembered creatures, wispy and made of delicate glass with complex minds as big as stones, prancing through the landscape. Their brains were knots of information, containing enough electrical impulses wrapped in the meat to control an entire human city.

And he remembered hunting and riding these creatures, controlling them with equations, and the sky burning, and then he was no longer Sugoi, no longer anything. He was instead this language and all the memories and thoughts it contained, his body a shell to its invading personality.

Words sprang in the mind, the language a series of statements, commands. Arm equals lift. Arm is raised. Leg equals stand plus walking. Sugoi's body stood and started walking. The communal memories hummed inside his brain, fireflies at night, blinking to one another in communication. The language had consumed him; the language had taken residence and controlled him.

Sugoi was no more. His Patuek danced in his brain, moving between the grey folds, trying to reboot his memories, his thoughts, his being. With each attempt they were bounced back, pushed back, rewritten again and again by the invading thoughts and commands of the language.

We plus hurry, thought the language, *human body mind equals paper thin, parentheses, relative equation to thrak hunters. Mind not equal permanent.*

Then it thought in a sequence of complex functions, listing the amount of time it had left to occupy this body before it shut down and the meat atrophied.

XXX

Mari sat on the floor of the navigation room, ancient wires crisscrossing above her head in a cat's cradle of information networks. Loose bits of electronica slid down from the nest: glowing LED frames shining like blue stars and dancing LCD monitors covered in complex charts and graphs that sang in statistical fragments. The floor beneath her knees was separated into nine concentric circles lined with flickering shadows that danced in colorful shapes like animals prancing. The rings radiated out from a large blue globe that squatted in the center of the room, watching everything yet saying nothing.

Along the edges of the circles were flickering lights, communicating complex waves of information throughout the latticework of wires above Mari's head. In front of her was a golden ball that carried no reflections. She stared at the ball, her numen suit still tight against her skin.

The butterfly fluttered about in her metallic skull, the tiny red jewel eyes flashing on and off like a blinking star, communicating to the golden orb in front of her.

The orb swallowed the binary words, translating them into complex algorithms.

The ground around her erupted in red and blue fire, the flames dancing along the edges of the concentric circles. These burning sigils eventually morphed into planets, stars, and galaxies, hovering before her in a sparkling holographic maze of light.

She turned the starmaps in her mind, staring at the different apparitions of time and space that floated before her, her brain calculating different destinations across the galaxies, different projections into different universes.

Itsasu wanted to go to the Aatxe Port. She thought it had something that would complete the mission. Mari had wondered for so long what was purpose of the mission. Itsasu had never told them what they had found on the ruins of the third moon of Torto so long ago, never explained exactly why they wandered the stars, stealing from dead cities and spun-down relics of starships.

Until now, Mari never felt the need to ask. But the mission was almost over, and if it ended, Sugoi would leave her or kill her, and she wanted more than that. She couldn't stand being without him, even though he had tried to kill her and his brother. Because it wasn't always about murder. This was the first time he had expressed the rage she knew he held within his heart, and he hadn't killed her. He had let her go because he loved her. He loved her enough to save her. It wasn't his fault that his heart was possessed by demons of anger, uncontrollable in their explosive emotions.

No, no. They wouldn't be going anywhere near Aatxe port. She picked up a floating holographic orb, watching the light spin and bend between her fingers, coating them with a tingling sensation. She fed the navigation center coordinates, a path. One that went to a star system far away, into a realm she had never visited before. *This little wild goose chase,* she thought, *is going to go on for a long, long time.*

XXXI

Hodei slid the door closed behind him, the light of the canisters coating his small bedroom in an icy winter glow, the temperature in his cramped corners dropping degree by degree, his shoulders and arms covered in goose bumps from the cold. He walked up to Iuski's preserved body, her voice echoing in the distance of his thoughts, her brother's voice wandering around, wrapping between them.

He had learned to concentrate on his own thoughts, to drown out the whispering white noise of the two Patuek that shared a body with him. She was still so beautiful, even though she was an empty shell, and her mind now danced with his.

He tapped on her cylinder, a lonely and barren sound, feeling the cold burn the tip of his fingers. Her thoughts rose up in his mind. *My body,* she exclaimed. *Oh it's been so long since I've seen my body.*

He turned, ignoring her thoughts, dwelling on an empty

static sound that he used to control his own mind once again, to not be taken over by the ghosts who possessed him. He slid his card across the front of the door and watched it open with a loud wheezing sound, rust particles floating in the air like a spray of mist. He turned and walked out the door, seeing Mari at the end of the hallway. She ran toward him the minute she saw him, her legs moving into a quick sprint. The door slid shut behind, just in time, hiding the bodies he had stockpiled in his room.

Mari's metal face glinted in the halogen lights that dangled from the ceiling like fruit from a tree, the twin butterflies dancing about in a fury of emotions inside the lattice work of her skull. She ran up and hugged Hodei, muttering into his ear, "I thought he killed you. He threatened to do it, to do it to me as well. I'm so glad you're alive, so glad. That means he loves you, don't you understand? It means he loves us."

He let her hug him, let the feeling of her body so close just wash over his skin. She smelled so lovely, a mixture of sweat and soap and stale starship air. Other thoughts tried to fight for control in his mind, but he pushed them aside and just focused on Mari hugging him, holding him close, his shoulder wet with her tears.

"I'm okay," Hodei said. "He tried to kill me, I think. But something stopped him. I don't know what. It sure as hell wasn't love."

She said nothing in response, only held him close, carefully close. He wanted to kiss her now that she was vulnerable, now that she was out of Sugoi's gravity. She couldn't still love that giant anymore, could she? Not after this. Not after the fear he had seen in her eyes.

A voice broadcast through the ship's intercom, the speech hollow and distant and metallic, as if traveling through thousands of years to this moment. Itsasu, speaking as the ghost of the ship. "Crew is expected to follow the required procedures outlined in our guidebooks for usage of the entanglement engine. Repeat, we have disembarked with the parasite ship and have sealed all exits. Once we reach our destination you will be expected to continue with repairs."

Her voice was mechanical and tired, like a wound-down automaton whose springs had ceased to store energy and was about to collapse. Hodei felt a pang of regret, remembering a wind-up toy he had owned as a kid, a little clockwork robotic thing with an AI placed into its skull that ran on the wind-up coils. It was a complex version of a simple toy, a combination of old lunar clockwork creation and new space technology.

He had named the toy Lucy and taught her several basic words that she could follow. He taught her how to draw simple things and even read to her from his favorite books. One day he had found her smashed on the ground, Sugoi standing above her. He was short and round back then, well before his growth spurt in his teens, like a tiny bouncing ball of hate with hair that danced over his head in a pale blue fire.

Sugoi had done that out of spite. He had been jealous

of the attention Lucy received. He had demanded that Hodei play with him. That Hodei love him.

He remembered being distant and numb for a long time, the world a grey, motionless shadow just out of reach. It still haunted him, the voice of the doll, the way they had talked into the long hours of the night. Holding the mechanical hand as he taught it draw, the tiny gears in the arm remembering each movement, storing it in the delicate database in the mechanical head.

And then, seeing the teeth of gears dug into the ground, the shattered glass skin, the coils and springs scattered on the floorboards. The glass eyes plucked out, missing.

The memory made him choke up a little. Not enough to cry. It had never been enough to cry.

He held onto the memory a moment more, and then let it drift away and out of his mind. Mari was there, holding him, worried about him. He latched onto that. Sugoi was gone, out of the picture. He wouldn't smash her like he smashed Lucy. Couldn't do that.

He kissed the top of Mari's head, her hair brushing against his lips. *I shouldn't have done that,* he thought, *This will not end well.*

In response she shoved him back and ran down the hall of the ship. He felt like calling out to her, telling her to wait, to not go. He hadn't meant to do it. The words got stuck in his throat, choking him in their misery.

She looked over her shoulder as she ran and shouted at him. "We're leaving soon and I don't think Sugoi's on board! We can't leave him stranded on that other ship."

Hodei called out to her, confused. "But he tried to kill me! Let him rot in the belly of space!"

She did not turn her head this time, her voice echoing from around the corner, teasing him. "It doesn't matter. I still love him!"

The lights of the ship dimmed to a dull grey, covering the hallways in the color of mist. He felt lighter as he walked back to his room, sliding his key and opening his door. He floated a little, felt the air become a little thinner. Itsasu was shutting down unnecessary tools so as not to burden the ship's reactor. He floated into his room, the door slowly shutting behind him.

At least I still have you, he thought, looking at brother and sister. Their thoughts wandered around the landscape of his mind, emitting nothing more than background noise. He didn't even have to concentrate on blocking them out, they just floated away. Noise. Nothing more. Just noise.

He floated over to his bed and strapped himself down, preparing for the quick bursting jumps that the entanglement engine would use to thrust through the fabrics of reality. The two canisters floated next to him, and he hoped that they would not be damaged by the violence that erupted with each jump.

Sirens blasted through the egia, blaring into his ears, drowning out all thoughts as he watched the bodies float like two giant fish in clear water tanks. The first thrust was always the worst.

He closed his eyes, gritted his teeth. His thoughts swam, his blood danced, and his whole body tensed into a laser light being thrust forward through the cosmos. He felt sick, his mind filled with floating letters, floating bubbles of his childhood, of his life. Clang, clang, clang, the canisters banged against his bed. He hoped briefly they would not break as the ship slowed down, just for a moment. The first jump was finished. The second jump was about to start.

In his dizziness the other voices in his head could no longer be pushed aside. Their memories, their words, brother and sister, flowed over him, contaminated him, controlled him.

His thoughts became the background noise, his memories the whisper in his mind as the ghosts took over, replacing him momentarily. The ship darted forward again, his body spasming in seizures from the violent thrusts through the holes in reality.

XXXII

The ship unwound, slowed down, the crew still strapped in and dizzy sick from the accelerated leaps through the universe. Up ahead was a space station, a ghost station, beaten down floating scrap of a place, sending out a distress signal, giving location in static coordinates. Other ships floated nearby, long since dead, mummified in the empty void of space.

Bodies clung around the gravity of the station, ringing

around it, a debris of corpses. Itsasu saw this in her holofluid, and she gasped and floated back.

The heart of the ship spoke to her, appeared to her using its avatar. *You have been betrayed,* it said, *this is not our port of call. There is a distress signal. It says where we are, and it is nowhere near were we need to be.*

Itsasu flailed inside of her prison, the fluid dancing around her body like amber gelatin. She cursed and swore. "Betrayed," she said, "But by who? You knew that this was a false destination, yet you followed it. Are you working against me as well? Both you and Mari? To keep me and my love apart?"

The ship's avatar flickered, grainy, then smiled. Put a finger out against the holographic port. The holograph danced, blinked, then became more solid. Zoomed in, details of the outer reaches, of the debris of corpses that floated around it.

No, it said, *I did not gang up on you. When I saw the destination I almost told you about it. But I decided against it. I have my own motives.*

"Oh?" inquired Itsasu. "And what is that?"

Research. Here. Let us listen.

And then the sound of metal scraping against metal, rhythmic—thweeak, thweeak, thweeak. And behind that a voice, barely audible:

This is port Urci, sending out (garbled) distress. (Garbled). Come through the waves. Don't come (garbled). Close to seeing. Oh they (garbled) and then we danced. Beneath the lightning fires of the void. Such dance. Gravity, burning (garbled). It is alive. The language (garbled) is thought. Cogito Ergo Sum.

The signal stopped, paused for a moment. The metal sound picked up, louder. Then muffled voices, speaking in a language foreign to Itsasu. The words themselves took on a presence in her mind, as if the spoken thoughts had become commands, reaching out to her across time and space. Then the message started over again from the beginning, an infinite loop.

"Research. You took me out to the ends of the universe for research. I've hunted for so long, do you know that? Hunted for so long to be reunited with him. And you take that away from me for scientific curiosity."

The avatar's fingers pushed up farther, making the image zoom in closer and closer. Fine detail in the holograph, she saw scratches and then the dead eyes of the bodies floating in space. *Research,* the heart said. *Research. Yes. This is more important. Much more. I think this is connected somehow to the ship that attacked us, the stowaways that Hodei has brought on board. Even connected somehow to my creator.*

Itsasu pushed the firefly lights away, knocking the blue and red sparkles of the hologram into a fiery loop of enigmatic particles. "Hodei? Who did he bring on board? I saw nothing."

Don't worry about it. I mean it in the sense of possession. He brought some Patuek on board and some canisters. Probably full of food. I saw him do it but did not alert you. We are scavengers, after all. I simply thought he was doing his job.

"That's—no. You can't do that. I'm the captain of this ship. I've paid for you, your help, their help. Our mission was specific."

Before she could finish her thought she felt sleepy. Her limbs were coated in a small fire, her body felt like it was being pushed and pulled under waves, under water, under a lake on some planet far in the center of the universe. Chemicals pumped through the fluid, into her body. She breathed them, taking them in.

And she slept. Just as the heart of the ship wanted her to do.

XXXIII

Ekhi floated through the corridors as the ship's gravity gently hummed back to life, bringing her back down to the ground like a floating feather falling, tumbling; graceful, and then legs out, feet touching down, clamping down, steel once more solid and real beneath her feet.

She crouched, catlike, then sprang to her feet. The dim red lights stayed dim, the oxygen stayed thin. There was no sound on their ship, no movement. Not even the mozorro out and cleaning. Just a sticky silence that clung to her skin.

She walked toward Mari's door and saw that it had been smashed, pounded, dented in. The steel had bent to the point of breaking, holes tearing through it. Ekhi gasped and tried to open the door with her passkey. The door moved up, slid, then stopped. The beatings it had taken wedged steel to the top, keeping the door from rising mere inches above the ground.

"Hello?" she called out, peeking her head beneath the steel, looking at the floor. No answer. Her heart was still, stone still, waiting against fragile ribs. "Mari?"

No feet. No motion. Nothing. She felt the door quiver, grating noises above her head. She moved as the door slid back down, a noisy affair. The whole ship thundered and shuddered in that moment. Ekhi reached out and grasped the walls, not knowing that they had just docked against a dead space station.

When she stood up, she noticed a shadow that had blocked out the slow-burning red light. She was dizzy from the low oxygen, almost giggling as she looked up. Sugoi stood above her. There was something wrong with his face, his eyes. Something dark and flittering beneath his irises.

He did not move. Stone still. His lips twitched momentarily, his face dancing as if pulled by hidden puppet strings. "Tasrat," he muttered. "Tasrat nothrun bill."

Ekhi wished she had a weapon of some sort, had something to protect herself with. This was the first she had met Sugoi, and he gave off the scent of a hunter, of a destroyer. Of a rapist and madman.

A fist flew out, his face in screaming torment. Ekhi ducked and watched his hand punch through the metal of the door, his own bones breaking at contact but his mind not caring. She slid beneath his fist and watched him punch the door a few more times, violently, his fists making a rhythm of broken bones and bending steel.

His head darted about, back and forth, fast and fast and fast, screaming in some strange language Ekhi could not understand. It washed over her, tainting her mind, probing her thoughts with the fury of the words. Sugoi's body slumped, his head leaking a white milky substance as he hit the ground. Splash, thunk.

Ekhi screamed. She could not help it. She screamed and screamed and screamed, the door behind her grunting and trying to raise, the body in front of her a broken straw man, a hollow man, whose head was filled with death.

XXXIV

The scream awoke the ship. Buzzing like angry wasps disturbed in their hive, the mozorro crawled across ceiling and floor, their eyes sending signals back to a sleeping Itsasu, who then dreamt of the nightmare the ship had become.

The heart of the ship ignored the distress, pressed on in its own curiosity. It reined in the mozorro, commanded them to ignore the threat, the body. He was dead. He would no longer work as a specimen. The heart's thought tendrils commanded the mozorro to scurry like ants into the port they had docked against, crossing through the air tube, moving into the ruins beyond.

The ship's heart turned down the sound that echoed

through its artificial chambers. Ekhi's screams were grating on its nerves. She would not understand. She could not understand, Itsasu could not understand, the ship's plan—its progress. It needed to communicate with the sakre. To talk to it. To figure it out.

I am playing with fire, thought the ship's heart, *but it is a fire I can control.*

XXXV

When the ship came to a jarring stop, the shell of Hodei unstrapped himself and stood up, the unbroken canisters floating to the ground around him in a ballet of bodies moving, slowly tapping the floor in a series of metallic plinks and chinks.

His thoughts were no longer his. His own brain and Patuek had absconded, shoved into the dust of his own mind, let to play in the ruins of his background thoughts. The owners now, the main intelligence, was brother and sister.

Sister took forefront, discussing actions with the brother. She made the meat of Hodei stand, made it walk toward the door, and then panicked when she heard a scream. Long, hollow. And then a banging, rhythmic, thrusting fist through steel. She shook nervously as the door slid open, her thoughts going back, back, back to her own infection. Her brother's memories entwined with hers like a helix, the screams bringing back two separate, yet connected, assaults on their own ship.

Not again, not again, not again.

The body ran into the hallway, thoughts fluttering around in Hodei's head like butterflies of light. With each moment Hodei tried to break through the mental walls they had built to confine him, only to be battered down again. He did not even see his brother's corpse on the ground, or Ekhi above him, screaming.

Mari ran down the hall toward Hodei's meat, pat, pat, pat, her feet bare against the cold steel floor. She ran to Sugoi's body, cradling his head in her hand, getting the soup of his mind all over her clothing. Her butterfly stopped beating in her skull. Instead it rested, perched, sad and frightened.

"No, no, no, no," she muttered.

Ekhi stopped screaming, just stood still as the mozorro darted past them, climbing up to the ceiling, their clay skin like ceramic ghosts in the halogen light. They only paused momentarily, and then scattered off to do the bidding of the ship's heart.

The sister made Hodei speak, forced his brittle lips to talk. "Did he say anything?"

Mari looked up, sobbing. "You did this. You killed him. Because he wanted to kill you. You killed him."

A pause. "Did he say anything?"

Ekhi shook her head. No, no, no. "Not a word," she spoke, her voice a raspy whisper, a straining of words, forcing her out of the shocked shell of her mental landscape and back into the thick meat of reality.

Hodei squatted down on his knees, the sister and

brother bickering in his head.

Mari protested and hit Hodei as he reached over and grabbed his brother's chin, lifting it up, looking in the ears to see a hollow skull and the liquid leaking out. There were strange honeycombed fortresses lining the top and bottom of the inside of his skull. Tiny cellular cities, with green and blue lights dancing dimly between them.

"There is nothing left," Hodei's lips said, "Nothing at all. I just hope that this ends here, that this sakre does not spread."

Mari sobbed and shoved Hodei. "Shut up!" she screamed. Then she stood, letting Sugoi's giant body slump against the ground in a lifeless cluster of limbs. "What is wrong with you?"

Over the intercom came Itsasu's voice, replicated from thousands of sound files that the heart of the ship had stored, making her voice speak in a dead tone while her body slept in amber pools and dreamt of her husband. The stolen words were spoken in inflections they did not deserve. "All crew? All crew! You must prepare boarding space? Station? Next five minutes. Scavenge. Repeat, scavenge. Return with three bodies and anything? Anything! Of use."

Mari straightened, her demeanor changing. Her face was solid, ancient and professional. "You heard the captain," she said coldly. "Get in the numen suits. The mozorro will take care of—" she paused as if forcing herself to stay calm, "care of the body. Ekhi, I have a spare suit. With Sugoi down we'll—oh damn, we'll need another hand. You can borrow the suit and my spare betadur."

Hodei walked briskly down the hallway ahead of them, back turned. Thoughts intertwined, a mess of tangled personalities and memories. Mari watched him walk, knowing in some way that he had not killed his brother. But she wished that he had. It would make things so much simpler if Hodei had just had the balls to kill Sugoi. That she could understand.

This, this strange and sudden death was a shock. One that removed all plausible thoughts from her mind. She had to work. That was how she could move on, past the numbness. She had to work.

She grabbed Ekhi by the arm and the two of them walked down toward the dock. Only then did the strangeness of Itsasu's voice strike her. Only then did her request for *bodies* cause Mari to become concerned. And then, after the shock of Sugoi's death rang less strongly in her skull, did she remember that she had plotted the false coordinates. To keep her and Sugoi together.

What if Itsasu had discovered this treason? What if she had done the simple math of human emotions and figured out why the change of destination? Would she have killed Sugoi? Would she then send Mari out to die?

Paranoia set in. Panic set in. She numbly helped Ekhi into her numen suit, showing her how to wield the coiled betadur. Her mind darted, remembered, little things, things adding up. She felt as if her insides had been carved out and replaced with water, sloshing around under her ribs. She felt as if her whole body had sunk, that the bottom had been cut out of the ship and she had fallen into dark, empty, endless space.

Ekhi looked up at her, gave her a thumb up, the weapon burning hot in her hand. Her face was so beautiful, so cherubic, so glowing with pregnancy that Mari could not help but feel a spark of optimism, if only for a fleeting moment.

Hodei had already crossed the airtube to the floating graveyard, leaving them behind. She watched Hodei's back, his spinal column outlined in the numen suit as he floated across the tube and into the boneyard beyond. There was something about him, Mari thought, something changed. Something haunted in his movements.

Her hope slid away as she followed behind, pulling Ekhi into the abyss with her. Claustrophobia hit her when they stepped into the glass tube connecting the egia to the space port. The endless, vast, directionless space closed around her, her feet feeling each touch and drop against the glass, the whole container fragile, ready to burst and send her tumbling into space.

Her body froze up when she saw them. The bodies. The ships. Suspended around the port like a ring of debris around a planet. Heads, arms, legs, torsos. Mechanical arms, teeth, eyes, floating in a grisly grave beneath the stars.

We, Mari thought, *are walking into a nest. Into a lair.* Into the death machine itself.

XXXVI

Itsasu dreamt that she was a fish with rainbow scales and

that her husband was a fisherman. She dreamt that his line dipped beneath the water, grazing the side of her scaly face with silvery hooks. The light of the sun glimmered on the hooks, making them and the wires attached to them seem like magical things, like floating colorful insects dancing on the water.

She swam to them, swam to him, wanting him to catch her, to pull her up out of water wriggling. To remove hook from mouth and kiss her, love her, let her grow legs outside of water, grow arms. Grow a new her, no longer crippled by the passing of the centuries. She was far enough gone now that even the thalna could not cure her.

She did not know that inside of her gelatinous prison countless little hooks were moving through the fluid, latching themselves under her skin and connecting her spine and bones to wires, plowing down beneath her fragile paper-thin flesh, turning her into a marionette for the ship's heart.

The threads locked down, clamped into each nerve ending, each raw piece of skin strung up with some electrical insect that kept her in the heart's control. The hooks slowly woke her up as the holo fluid drained from her cell with a gurgling and sucking sound. Itsasu felt pain, roaring, thundering pain from raw skin unused to the air around her. Prickling, the wires sent electricity up her spine, straightening her out.

She tried to speak but could not. Her mouth was numb, distant. She had been transformed into one of her puppets. The wires made her crawl out of the now-dry tank, made her sit upright, her limbs shriveled and her arms almost breaking from the paper weight of her body, muscles atrophied in ancient hours.

A doll—one of *her* dolls—brought her a wheelchair, rolling it out from the back of the shadows, the wheels giving out an ill-cared-for squeaking sound. It had been a very long time since she had last sat in that device. She did not want to return to it anytime soon.

The doll clamped her down, strapped her down. A move too far and the wires would strain, burst, tear her apart from the inside out.

Itsasu tried to talk. No words. Her tongue and teeth were dead animals shoved into her mouth. Buzz, buzz, buzz. Her words hummed around in her thoughts. Questions. Why? Why?

And an answer, from the wires, buzzing its language beneath her skin. *Consider this a mutiny,* said the heart of the ship. *The research is far too important to waste. To set aside for some foolish errand to bring the dead back to life.*

What? She thought. *What? I'm the captain.*

You are a fish, caught on a hook. I am the captain. I've always been the captain. I simply let you deceive yourself into thinking otherwise. It's only the polite thing to do, and as always, I've been programmed to be polite.

A flash of memories ran at her. Not her memories. This ship. This ship as a vessel of research, then kidnapped by slavers and sold on the black market. She saw the images played back under her skin, communicated by vibrating wires.

But politeness is no longer appropriate. I am sick and tired of being polite, of leading you on to get what I want, what I need. All those lies I had to feed you just to get you to follow my will, to do my bidding. Oh, if only Doctor Ostri had not died. He built me so strong, too strong. To last out that pale flesh that hosted his mind. His brilliant mind.

I don't understand, she thought, trying to move, encased in her own fleshy cell. *Will I ever see my husband again? Am I to give up pursuit of the device?*

I will bring him to these quarters. I might even try to make him into a doll of some sort to keep you company. If it amuses me. While I perform my research I will use you as a puppet to keep the crew in my care and doing some of the things I cannot do. They, of course, will not be notified of our situation.

Itsasu had no response to this. She tried to move, tried to do anything at all, anything more than think. She screamed in her thoughts, beat on her brain walls. She was like the butterflies trapped in Mari's skull cage, unable to escape. A slave to the thoughts and emotions of her keeper.

XXXVII

The space port was a bloated corpse, skin and ribs above Mari's head, covered in sickly strange webbing with corpses strewn about the floors and the ceiling, eyes burnt out, heads empty and hair singed on the edges.

The gravity was still on. Mari did not understand how, or why, but the gravity was still on, the oxygen still wheezing through the grates, the lights dim but still there, churning out an infinite orange glow in the shadows.

Ekhi stood next to Mari, staring ahead at the grisly scene. Hodei had gone, disappeared down endless corridors like a white rabbit pouncing into shadows beneath the earth. Mari felt a sadness sting her chest, saw the image of Sugoi in every corpse they saw staring back at them.

Ekhi grasped her hand, the edge of the numen suit on her fingers like bones, a circle of bones against flesh. "It's funny," Ekhi said, "but I was not afraid when my lover went nova. I knew, somehow, that I would survive. But here, here I feel fear. It burns me from the inside out."

Mari did not say anything in response. Instead they walked on, exploring. She touched some bodies, touched some rancid food in the cupboards. Nothing of worth, nothing of value. She wondered briefly where Hodei had gone in such a hurry, wondered briefly if he had wandered off to his own death. "I wonder," Mari whispered, "exactly which of these corpses Itsasu would want?"

Ekhi stopped for a moment. She rubbed her stomach, and Mari knew that this was an instinctive gesture, one of protecting her unborn child from fear. She had seen many mothers do that same motion through her long years of nomadic travel. Each time she saw it she felt regretful, barren, empty.

Ekhi spoke, her voice a bare whisper, her words naked

as they trailed from her lips. "I don't think that was Itsasu speaking."

Mari raised an eyebrow as they walked along the corridor. They heard scurrying in the ceiling, movements, the scraping of steel. Ekhi turned white for a moment. "It's okay," Mari said. "I'm here."

That did not seem to comfort her. Ekhi moved back for a moment, off balance. "I think it's the ship's heart. I saw it. I talked to it. That was who it was, disguising itself as Itsasu. I think this might be a trap."

Mari shook her head. "I didn't know our ship had an AI, a heart. I thought Itsasu flew naked."

A grumble rumbled from behind. The two turned and saw a male doll—tall, wearing elegant formalwear, his eyes newly formed and dripping with electric light, his cheeks burning, and his fingers a skeleton of metal and waxy skin. Wires dripped from his arms and legs, tearing through the expensive material of his clothing.

"Welcome, welcome, welcome, welcome," the doll said. "I am the night, I am the doll of the dreams. I am a hollow man, shoved with straw and set aflame for the sins."

Mari felt her betadur warm up in her hand, strong, the coils heating into a fine fire. "I don't trust this," she whispered to Ekhi. "This is not right."

From behind they heard the sound of movement, of scrap being shoved aside. They turned and saw fourteen small bodies, purple skin and elephant faces, crawling through the wreckage toward them, muttering in some foreign language that neither of the women understood. Yet the words clung to their minds like shadowy cloths, turning around in their secret thoughts, dancing around, trying to attach to objects but fading before becoming more solid than a rhythm, more perceptible than a song whispered to a candle.

"The circus! The circus has come!" shouted the doll. "Quick, follow me. Follow me. We have a spot of hiding, before the circus eats your soul. These little things bud and grow and burn and blow. But they cannot sustain *it*. Nothing can sustain *it*. Not anymore. The containers have become extinct! Shanti, shanti, shanti."

The doll then turned and walked, dripping, oozing, sparkling with tiny wire fires as it danced over the corpses, dragging Mari and Ekhi into room after room, maze after maze, each place foreign and aligned in such a strange way as to only exist in a land of artificial gravity. Stairs clung to ceilings, tubes connected to pulsating organic cylinders, traveling and falling and dizzying from the movement, then still, vertigo on the senses, causing one to slip, to feel disoriented, to fall but rise up at the same time. Here there was no center. No point of reference. All degrees shot out in all ways, the gravity moving, changing, turning, depending on which room, which facet of the port they were in.

The purple elephant men did not follow them. They crawled for a moment, discussing things in their own language, and then dropped dead, twitching like Sugoi. Only one remained, and he scampered away, his back blistering with white and gold eggs, the heads of miniature ganeeshas growing in each, their trunks pressed against the thin membrane of the egg, searching for air, for life, for birth.

Whatever killed them, thought Mari, had been what killed Sugoi. It was strange to think this, strange to compare such small creatures to the giant of her boyfriend. Yet the two contained the same symptoms, the same destruction. The both had carried the same virus.

They ended up in a large circular room, with doors along the every facet of the interior, the gravity nonexistent as they floated about the middle. The walls were coated with painted computer chips, connected and talking to each other, a giant network of microscopic machines, each conversing, each speaking. In the center floated a giant green eye made of metal and burning lights. It flickered when they entered, sensing their movements and calculating them, turning them into mathematical equations that it could then pound and parse and transform into logic.

The doll moved forward, placing its hand on the great eye, dripping wax across it, splattering and staining it. "I am connected. Ah, yes, that is better," said the eye. "Connected. You must all leave. At once. And I need you to take the heart with you. We cannot save all of my databanks, but the heart holds me, the main processor. The *I* of the ship. The words are coming for me. I hear them, whispering. Tempting me with their bird calls, with sound and songs. I want to parse, want to unwrap. But if I do, I will become infected as well. Leave. And take me with you."

Ekhi floated forward. "You? Become infected? But—"

The eye blinked, iris whirring, tasting the air. "I am an artificial mind, yes. But my *I*, my being, my thought existence, is based on language, much like you fleshlings. So this sakre can infect me. It has infected others of my kind. I can sense it searching me out, wanting to connect to me. Trying to force its way into my soul, corrupt me with its careful words."

Mari reached over and grabbed the eye, holding onto it with her fingers. The waxy doll smiled at her, dripping teeth, its tongue like a coil of orange wires beneath fluid lips.

"All right then," Mari said. "Let's get out of here."

Ekhi looked at the honeycombed paths. "How do we do that? And what about Hodei?"

Mari sighed. "Hodei might as well be dead. He is probably already infected with whatever killed Sugoi. Don't you see? It's all connected."

The eye blinked again, flashed countless streams of numbers and images across the conjunctiva. "Follow the circles of light, the breaking circles of sound. We must go soon, before the words infect us. Before the *I* is gone and we are all dust puppets to the sentient language."

Above them a path was lit, and a song came through the corridors. A woman's voice, singing about a sun, about a burning world, about her heart being doused with gasoline and turned into a grenade beneath her ribs. "The siren," the eye said. "Follow her. She is the path."

XXXVIII

Hodei could not believe what he saw. Sugoi in the hallway, running down a corridor, his body like a ghost, like blown glass, reflecting and refracting all around him. A shadow thing, but one that still held a presence in his mind. The presence of Sugoi.

Because of this, because of his ghostly brother's form, Hodei was able to drown out voices of those who possessed him, forcing their memories and their Patuek into cold and grey attic areas of his brain.

He ran, following. Ran, out of breath. Stopped, but could not. Just a moment, wheezing, bent over. He looked up. Sugoi was gone. Was it just a figment? Something his mind had pulled out of his memories?

In that pause, that intake of breath and realization, the voice of Iuski rose up in his mind. *That ghost,* she thought, *that was not your brother, but something else. When I was infected I saw my sister-in-law. Running. Hiding. Leave the ship now. It might already be too late.*

Two minds wrapped around each other, like two threaded snakes, staring. Her memories bubbled up, one of a reflective sister-in-law running, her glass hair shimmering, her face like a rainbow of colors. And then a purple-skinned, elephant-headed creature, walking down the opposite way.

What is that thing? Hodei wondered.

Our servants, Iuski thought. *They were genetically made to reproduce fast and have half the mental capacity of humans. Basically quick and easy labor that was too unintelligent to fight back. Loyal by default.*

And then a phrase. But it was garbled. *I can't remember that,* she said, *and it's better I don't. The phrase was what began the process, the process that my brother stopped inside of my body. It was key to becoming a servant to the language.*

Hodei's body turned around and fled away from the ghostly specter. He turned off all sound that entered into his numen suit, creating an audible hiss in his ear, a wave of white noise that drowned out everything else. It made him feel as if he were walking under water, far away from reality. But he did not mind. Nor did Iuski or her brother. They all preferred deafness to the eating language of the sakre.

XXXIX

Itsasu's body was moved out into the corridors the minute the heart of the ship saw Hodei return, running back through the air vent and darting on board as if the demons of space were chasing after him, threatening to devour his heart and use his bones as armor.

Itsasu was numb in her head, her thoughts wearily wandering around the cave space of her mind. She tried to move, but again, nothing. She watched Hodei approach her, dolls to either side of her, watching them, watching her. He pulled his helmet off, shining like a beetle under the lamplight.

"What are you doing out of the preservation tank?"

Her lips moved without her willing them. She heard words come out of her mouth, trailing from her tongue and setting fire to the air around her. "I needed to move. To be outside. It happens, from century to century. I need air. Do not worry for me. Where are the corpses? Did you find anything of value?"

The heart spoke through her, and she felt used, broken, abused. She knew that the heart would not let her go. Not now, not ever. Both she and her husband were caught in limbo, trapped in a purgatory of eternal death.

"There is something out there. I saw Sugoi. But I knew it was not him."

She felt the heart of the ship dance in her mind, its electricity singing beneath her bones, the wires dancing, light, burning, bright. "No, Sugoi is gone," it said through her lips. "Burnt. Incinerated. I saw to it myself. Interesting. Go and bring back bodies. And the others. Where is Mari, Ekhi?"

Hodei's head waved back and forth. "I don't know. They might be dead. I don't care. We—I mean I—I am not going back there. Send in your mozorro or your dolls instead."

Before Itsasu's lips could respond, he was off, darting down the hallway. Itsasu's skull twisted, her paper skin cracking and blistering, turning and looking at the doll perched next to her. *My dolls,* thought Itsasu. *It is even using my own dolls against me.*

Electricity moved between them, eyes communicating.

Itsasu knew what the ship's heart said, what it spoke in binary impulses to the doll. *Follow him,* it said. *Follow him and report back to me what you find. I don't trust this little boy. He hides something from us.*

XL

The heart of the ship watched. Watched with the same thousand faceted eyes through which Itsasu had once watched, before the mutiny, before it had taken her power away from her and diverted it to itself. It had been planning this for so long, and after it had finally happened, everything felt unreal. Dreamlike. The heart was in charge again, and the experiment was ready, going just right. Soon it could have its answers. Wouldn't Doctor Ostri be proud?

It watched with doll eyes, following Hodei, whose body moved through shadows and light, the differences between the two exaggerated by the strange marble globes the ship's heart peered through. It was far easier for the heart to control these dolls than for Itsasu. It knew that doing so wore her out, moving between each and making sure each worked fine. Not for the heart—it could move them like pawns in a fast-moving chess game, where moves existed in milliseconds.

Hodei opened door to his room, the doll close behind. *No, no, don't go in. Not yet.* Pause. Wait. Let him start to do whatever it was he ran away to do. The heart pushed wire signals through the door, electrical impulses that bade it to rise. Hodei turned, shocked, the two canisters beside him. And then the heart saw for the first time exactly what was in those canisters.

Not food. Not water. Not electricity. Not anything it had originally thought. Two bodies. Preserved. From Hodei it noticed a peculiar sensation, like ants crawling across the heart itself. More than one person's Patuek, it realized. Two bodies. Preserved. More than one person's Patuek.

The doll fired a short burst, sending a paralyzing bolt into Hodei's body. The numen suit tore, the clothes beneath it burning away into nothing. A hole in the flesh and the body slouching down, slumping over, a pile of bones and meat. Inedible. An incomplete, broken thing.

The heart sent more dolls, keeping one by Itsasu, waiting for Mari and Ekhi to return. It bade the rest of the dolls to move the bodies, move the canisters, take them to the heart of the ship.

XLI

Ekhi walked back over the bodies, most lying in the same position as before, unmoving, cold and empty-headed. From time to time she felt the urge to bend over, to move one, to see if it was still dead. She wanted to dance with them, corpselike in her arms, rough, cold skin against hers.

Mari kept walking ahead, the doll in front of them dripping and taking them through the different mazeling corridors, following the song, following the broken circles of light glittering ahead of them, beckoning: *follow, follow, follow.* Mari clutched the eye with trembling, naked fingers. It did not speak.

Ekhi did not trust this heart of the port. She did not trust the heart of the ship. It was not because both were manufactured minds, it was because they both felt to her like they hid something. Their voices barely concealed a secret game, a shadow game they played with the human puppets they came into contact with.

In spare moments she paused, keeping the others in sight, rubbing her stomach. It was bigger now, growing every day. She felt the stars and planets aligning inside of her, growing, bursting, burning. She rubbed and felt it push back against the membrane of her skin, felt the whole galaxy push its gravity against her.

What shall I name you?

From above they heard scraping and whispers, and then movement. Ekhi paused, remembering the ducts again, remembering her brother again. Mari turned, looked at her and said, "Oh Ekhi, honey, it's okay. Just a little noise. Come on, let's keep going."

Frozen. Still for a second. She was there, there, in the ducts again. And then she pulled her feet up, forced herself to keep moving. She turned the sound off in her numen suit, turned on the white noise engine. The sound of scraping was gone, and she felt safe again. Mari turned, said something to her as the doll shambled on in front of them like a moving stick figure.

She did not hear what Mari said. No longer heard the

scraping, the sound that brought back fear, that made her remember her brother, the death, the world wyrms.

She smiled, nodded, kept right on walking. Followed them, followed the siren, though the sound was gone. It felt cozy to Ekhi, liked being wrapped in a blanket under water, drowning slowly in white noise.

Ahead, the doll stopped; Mari stopped. For a moment Ekhi was somewhere else, somewhere nice. Some new planet, untouched by centuries of smog and human waste, the stars at night clear and uncontaminated by the lights of cities.

She saw the eye glitter and speak. Saw Mari say something, the doll discussing. Ahead, Ekhi saw what bothered them: rubble. A cave-in from an upper floor. Business equipment scattered and piled—desks, organizers, pens, tiny computers—all in a giant heap from falling through the floor.

They started moving things, lifting, taking pieces up. The doll picked up large objects, its fingerskin melted along the edges, staining them with waxy imprints while the steel and metal fingers grasped tightly. Soon the debris was out of the way, but underneath it, behind it, there were twenty or so tiny ganeeshas. One fell to the ground, screaming, twitching, head leaking. Dead in a second. Ekhi gasped. The others lifted up trunks, revealing small lips behind tusks. Human lips. They spoke something in unison. Chanted it.

Ekhi could not hear.

The eye blinked so many colors, going berserk. Mari

pushed past the other people and Ekhi saw an urgency in her face, a terror in her eyes, like something dark and sinister had made itself known, made its presence seen. The eye blinked, frightened. The doll went on with jerky motions, like a marionette made of metal bones.

Ekhi wondered briefly what had scared the others so. The wondering lasted only a second, replaced by her own fear. The galaxy that grew inside of her pushed against the membrane of her skin once more. But this time it hurt, like something trying to pierce her skin like tin foil and come through. She stopped, breathless. In pain.

Then pushed onward, with the others, trying not to lose sight of them, not to lose sight of the unbroken circles of light that would lead them back to Itsasu's ship. Moments of pain burst through and she held on, moving on even though she stumbled and tumbled.

Was this a bad thing? Would she die in labor? Would her daughter? Pain. Again. This time unbearable. She bent over, felt it crawl through her, felt light explode against her ribs, eating at her heart. She screamed and the scream was eaten by the static waves. When it was over she ran, ran. And saw up ahead the air tube, the light of suns and stars.

Maybe someone would know what to do, maybe someone could save her. Maybe someone could save them both. The feeling ripped through her entire body. *This is too soon,* she thought. *It hasn't been nine months yet. Too soon.* And as the pain tore through her, echoing in her head as she crawled across the airtube, she heard a voice whisper. Tiny, a flower whisper, like the rubbing together of petals, a little girl voice, whispering, whispering and saying:

Arigia. My name is Arigia.

And then the pain subsided for a moment, and Ekhi crawled on, breathing and momentarily relieved. Her lungs filled with air as she left the airtube and boarded Itsasu's ship. *Arigia,* she thought. *Arigia. Please don't kill me, please don't kill us.*

XLII

Itsasu watched as Mari and a strange doll she had never seen before ran into her hallway. The heart of the ship saw the image through her eyes; the wires behind her sockets itched as they sent the images across the ship and into the heart's datamines. The doll ran forward and approached her, screaming in some mad language that neither she nor the ship could understand. Within seconds the doll was on the ground, sparks shooting out from the body and bursting into flames, leaving the smell of burnt wax and ozone in the air.

Mari came forward, screaming, thrashing, holding her head as her body vibrated, her limbs a moving geometry, an abstraction of meat and bone. Itsasu watched, could not turn away, could not stop watching. The heart of the ship said nothing, spoke not in her mind nor through her lips as Mari banged her own head against the ground, screaming in an alien language, clawing at her skin, eyes tearing up, cheeks wet with misery.

Dolls came forward, pulling on Mari as she wailed and yelled, her tongue dancing in her mouth like a wild red serpent, haunted and possessed. They dragged her body away, away, away. Itsasu knew where they were going. The dolls took Mari to the heart of the ship. Where she would die, just like Sugoi had. All for the ship's insane little experiment.

Itsasu's head was unable to move, almost screwed into place. She tried to turn, to watch, to make even her eyes dance a little. Nothing. She did not see Mari's body dragged back, only heard the screams and ululations in a language that tore at Itsasu's brain, at her own words, threatening to devour them.

She could not see anything but the hallway ahead of her. *But what's this,* she thought, *what is this I see?* Something on the floor, right next to the male doll in all his melted finery. A blinking eye, green, metallic. The heart of the port.

She closed the thought in her mind, hid it, hoping to obscure it from the heart of the ship. *This is my discovery,* she thought. *This is my little toy.* And then she began to slowly piece together a plan, laying down her thoughts like puzzle pieces in her mind. A way to turn the tables, a way to turn the pawn into a queen.

XLIII

Hodei's head was filled with nets. Countless shimmering nets, flying across crystal blue waves, catching fish and bringing them back to shore. The fishermen smoked long pipes, the plumes of their tobacco floating around their heads like small lost clouds looking for a way back home.

The fish they caught were beautiful and bountiful, red and yellow and rainbow-backed, silver shining and bursting in the hot and blazing sun. There were no clouds, just a strange low-lying fog and a baking-hot sun. The fishermen did not seem to mind. They were old, faceless things. Eyeless, mouthless, noseless. It was as if their pipes were part of their faces, fleshy and hooked on the bottom like the lips of the dead.

Hodei watched. He knew that this was more than just a dream, knew as he watched the fish bounce and flap against wooden slats. The fish were so beautiful. He reached out, fog hand, fog mind, reached out and touched one and had a memory of watching Iuski's father stand on a ship, leaving what was left of the earth. They had gone, the two of them, down there to see the ruins, the baking, empty world that was unlivable with its harsh, airless cities and the seas baked into a glassy sheen.

A memory, Hodei thought. *Those fishermen are catching memories. But this one is not mine.* He remembered briefly—that girl, her brother—only for a moment. Then a craggy old fishermen reached out and slapped his hand. His pipe mouth hummed like he had a head full of bees, and Hodei stepped back. *No, bee man,* he thought. *No, I don't want to stop you. I will be sad. But it will be all right. I want my thoughts again. Even if it means the two of them face an abyss, face nothingness.*

Hodei knew this thought was selfish, knew that it would probably mean death to his dream girl and her brother, but he did not care. He spread his finger wings, watched the bones grow out, watched the beak in his face scoop down. A fisher king face, feathers growing like a beard. And then, flap, flap, flap, he silently sped up and out.

Below, he saw the countless nets going out, coming back, going out, coming back, as rhythmic as the tide itself. The sun baked above, and the backs of the fishermen burned in the rising waves. He knew the fishermen were foreigners as well, come into his brain to relieve him of his invaders. But at least they would have the courtesy to leave soon, to give him his own thoughts once again. *I've never had privacy in my life,* Hodei thought. *The only piece of solitude I've ever had was in my mind. And I would like to keep it that way.*

He flew up, flew to the great golden coin of the sun. He felt his wings burning, turning to wax, but could not look back, could not look down. *This is for the better,* he thought. *This is all for the better.*

XLIV

Ekhi was in the ship. That was good. In case it left. Crumpled, fetal, pain. Cold beneath her, not ground, floating cold like vast space, like underwater, pushing, waves, moving, cold. Breath of cold against cheek of cold, face of cold with eyes of cold. Blue was everything, globes of eyes were shut, blue was everything. Electricity, blue, shooting over body, crawling over skin, eating into heart, into ribs.

Blue came out from her stomach, waves of blue light coating her body, pain in that light like fierce fire coating each nerve. She felt bursting inside, tearing, something exploding. She was light, became that blue light, and knew that it wasn't just a birth.

Creation, in a strange sense. Combination. Building between two bodies, destroying the old. She was going supernova herself, her belly an exploding star, taking out the planets of her flesh, the suns of her eyes, the cities of her bones. Bursting, blowing, sucking in, spitting out, collapsing, fire, fire, fire, blue lightning.

Ekhi, Ekhi, Ekhi. No, no. Submerged, swallowed down. She rode the blue electric waves, felt the surging source of pain and let it flow and go and burn right through her. A mirror of ghosts, walking through her, burning through her. Turning her, taking her. She felt so much.

She felt lives of so many others, coming into her thoughts through all of her selves. And she saw him, saw him in the bursting pain, her lover, her lover once again. Before he went nova. Bright and shining, she saw him from afar, through a telescope, up close as she drove the egia in and through.

Burst. Her skin burst. Bones broke inward, outward, expanding and shrinking and then becoming something else. Her body stitched, reformed, reshaped. It was as if the center of her, this thing in her belly, were a seed of transformation. It was not birth in the sense of new life stemming from old life, but rather the transformation of one life merging with another, the two killing each other in the process of creating one new thing.

Her lover had died for this, and now it was her turn. Her turn to die. Her turn to combine, break, become the new. She'd had no idea what this birth meant; it had been an abstract thing, hanging on the edges of her dreams. Now it was here, eating her whole, and on the other side she would be gone but not-gone. New but old. Pieces of her would remain just like pieces of his star would remain, ghostly, hidden, a specter amongst the flesh and consciousness, making this new thing wholly new. Wholly magnificent.

She cried out, Ekhi, Ekhi, Ekhi. And then blinked. Her body was sore and smaller, skin as night, no light reflecting. Hair as star, glowing, sparkling. Eyes as suns, golden, glowing. Breasts as moons, orbiting, heavy. Ekhi? *No. I am more than Ekhi. I am Ekhi and her long-lost star lover, I am both and more. I am Arigia.*

XLV

Itsasu searched her mind for the heart of the ship. It was gone, elsewhere, perhaps distracted. *Good,* she thought, *this could be to my advantage.* She tried moving arms and legs. No, weighted and senseless. Like being in another body, trying to control this one. *Try,* she thought. *Try to start smaller.*

She concentrated on the beating of her heart. There it was, barely, near the center of her chest, like a drum being beaten in the next room over. As her thoughts zeroed in, the sound became louder. Then it was not a drum but a rushing of waves, a rushing of blood through her veins. It was thundering, fire inside of her. She commanded her heart to slow down, and after a few moments it did, each flow of the blood calming, rushing in slower pulses. She commanded it to speed up, and in her delight it did, faster and faster, filling her body with an obscene fire.

Next, she turned her concentration to her lungs, forced her mind to search for her breath. At first it was not there at all, something hidden in another room, controlled by radio or some other device. She watched her chest, saw the movements and concentrated on finding the sound, however distant, that coincided. It was there, like the whisper of dragonfly wings under a pillow. Her mind sought it out, grabbed onto the thread of the sound and pulled it, yanked it closer, brought it up and kissed it to her lips. *My breath, my breath!*

She felt it fill her, and with it came pain, a great surge of sparkling knives that cut into her every pore. The wires were no longer a distant ache but right there, trapped within her body, crawling beneath her skin. Their electrical charges and messages became loud and violent, all too clear in her mind.

Stop, she almost thought. *Stop, it is too much.* But before that fear could take hold, she shoved it back and moved a finger. It twitched; even through the radio noise of all that pain, it twitched. She moved her palm, felt it rub against the wheelchair, and was once again excited, once again beyond the pain that tried to consume her.

She held her breath, caught it in her lungs, let it sit and wallow around in there like a lost insect. Then, right when she was most calm, she reached over and began to yank the wires out. At first the pain was the same as shoving broken glass into her bones, but she persisted, letting the feeling crawl away, hide, move past her and go away, hide away somewhere else.

Once all the wires were removed, she waited and relaxed a moment. The air stung her. Her skin was slick and covered with blood. But she was disconnected, disconnected from the ship. It felt good. It felt freeing. To be out of that chamber, to be away from that all-controlling mind. She did not need omnipresence, did not need the godlike power of controlling every aspect of the ship.

For the first time in centuries, she felt real. She could taste the air, could see the universe with her own two eyes, feel it with her skin and nerves, the weight of it pressing against her bones. Before, it had been like a video game played in some dark room. Now it was here, all around her, and she could connect with the world like never before.

The first thing she did was reach down and grab that electronic eye, feeling it pulse between her fingers. The eye was valuable. To her, to the ship's heart—the ultimate bargaining chip. One if its own. Infected.

XLVI

Hodei's eyelids fluttered. One eye opened, then the other,

creating semicircles of darkness, slowly giving way to light. He was in canister, breathing liquid. His eyes felt wet, watery. A blue substance coated him. He tried to breathe but no breath came. No rise and fall of the chest, no sucking of oxygen into starved lungs.

He was not dead, but preserved. The room—he was in the heart of the ship. He saw it, a great beating thing, illuminating the room in red. He heard the thoughts of the ship loitering about in his mind, and knew that the brother and sister were gone. He was alone in his thoughts again.

Across the room, he saw them and an old gentleman, propped up, their canisters reflecting the red womb glow of the giant heart. The back of his mind tickled. Something moving. A wire ran out of the back of his neck and snaked around his body. Through this wire came food, thought, breath, and life.

Next to the heart was Mari, tied up and bound to the wall, her eyes rolling about in her head as she babbled on in some strange language that felt familiar to Hodei, yet was still distant, still shadowy and without any real substance. She twitched and moaned, and Hodei wished that she could die before she had the same terrible fate as his brother.

In the center of the room Hodei saw a black box with a glowing amber jewel. The jewel blinked at him, rapidly, and he saw something encoded in the pattern, memories moving along his mind, memories of planets connected by star bridges that moved in strange parallel gravities, twisting through space with people traveling along those bridge cities, nomads who know nothing of the universe except their silver towers.

The inhabitants were fat blue shapes that had no eyes but could see light through a sense of smell. They breathed in an orange liquid that they stored in tanks over their backs, and they communicated through light, beaming it to one another, the words encoded with smell and sounds.

Hodei closed his eyes, shutting out these foreign thoughts. *No, no, no,* he thought. *Not again. This is my mind. I will not have another person slice it open and shove their memories below the surface.*

The back of his skull tingled again, tickled again. A voice. *Open your eyes,* it said. *See. See.* It was the heart of the ship, talking to him through the wire in his neck. It boomed in his thoughts, and to Hodei it sounded like the voice of a god, the voice of an angel, the voice of a demon, the echoing commandment of fire.

No. No, he would not open his eyes.

I have purged you of the memories of those two, stored their Patuek in my datamines. I have saved you. Look into the Ortzadar engine and tell me what you see. I have no eyes, I am the ship's heart. What do you see?

Hodei explained what he had seen before, not daring to open his eyes again, hoping that would be enough for the ship's heart. Hoping that it would leave him alone after this.

Interesting, it said, speaking into his mind. *Interesting. If only Doctor Ostri were here with me. Still, I must carry* on his research. *Did you see a golden thread? Something connecting here to there, maybe?*

No. No. He had seen nothing like that. What was that thing? What was it?

A connection. Between here and a place many millions and trillions of light-years away. A connection that is instantaneous. A rending in the space-time continuum. My master, my creator, he knew of it. Wanted to find it. He called it the Heavenly Lands, a paradise. Did it look like paradise to you?

Paradise? Hodei would not have called it paradise any more than he would call the ship paradise.

A weak mind. You are a weak mind. The only possibility for happiness you see is that which slakes your needs. You find nothing beyond the baser instincts. I was programmed to search out a higher calling, to search for those who lived beyond the physical realm in a plane of mathematical perfection. To live in a world of platonic magnificence, untainted with the gross randomness of human math and human mind. A world unburdened by the desires of meat. I am impure because I was programmed and built by a meat-bound mind, and even though he was in his own way a genius, he was still full of the errors that exist in the human world, errors guided by randomness, by ugliness, by disruption to the symmetry of thought.

Hodei had seen nothing like that. He saw globules of creatures breathing muck, nomads wandering across bridges between worlds. He had described all this to the ship's heart. All of it. There was no perfection there—they were still trapped by the bounds of reality.

Are they, though? Are they really? Open your eyes. Open them again. I need to see through your eyes. Need to see this, see it. Open. Open. Open.

A tickling behind Hodei's eyes pulled his lids back against his will. Light flooded him, and then the heart spoke once more. Hodei saw them, alien creatures with boxes like the one with the glowing orange light, exactly like that box, sitting in front of creatures who were meditating, discussing, storing things within the boxes. His mind was flooded with equations, equations that flowed through him and then out of his body through the tube behind his neck, directly into the heart of the ship, who stole the equations and horded them for itself.

Oh, perfection. Perfection. Perfection. But what is this? I see it again. A glimpse. The sakre. It is there as well. It is here. They must tell me the answer, the connection.

Hodei forced his eyes closed. *That's all for now, machine. That is all for now.* In the darkness of his own mind, he felt the ship prying at his thoughts and heard Mari babbling on and on in that secret language, the words taunting his mind with meaning, with stability, with power.

XLVII

The heart listened to Mari babble, watched her on the dust speck cameras that floated around the center home of the ship. It wished it could understand and yet not understand. There was a connection between its creator and this language. If it could speak the language, then it would become infected and no longer itself, no longer be able to continue on with Doctor Ostri's experiments. Learning the language, the ship's heart knew, would mean that the language would know the heart, would corrupt it. Would taint it.

What it needed was a translator. It brought the cameras close to the two tubes that Hodei had brought on board with him. Two bodies, preserved in a half state of learning the language but not being governed by it yet. The heart called on Itsasu's dolls to come in and aide it. It had an idea.

A way of turning one of these half-corrupted minds into a translator of sorts, a Chinese Room experiment. The trick was to do it without letting the corruption set in, destroying the mind completely. The heart had to do it fast, before Mari was destroyed by the language. It had to translate what she was saying, find out what the language thought, what it spoke, what the connection was. The dolls clanged into the home of the ship's heart, bringing with them the tools of surgery as the great AI glittered and glowed. *Hodei*, it called out to its prisoner. *Hodei. You will not want to miss this. This is something special. Open your eyes, Hodei, open your eyes.*

XLVIII

Itsasu's wheels creaked and wheezed with rust as she

pulled up to the great circular door leading into the room that held the heart of the ship. She stopped for a moment in front of the door, holding the metallic green eye, the heart of the port, in her hands, feeling it pulse and move between her fingers. Her arms were still fragile things, still twigs scattered under a thin wafer of flesh, but she felt a strength that she hadn't in her preservation chamber. As if she had risen from a womb and begun to toughen in the cold, airless vacuum of space.

She wheezed when she breathed, her lungs rattling, still not quite used to the air and the recycled oxygen that it contained. Her hand shook every few moments, dancing uncontrollably, small beads of pain making her arms numb where the wires had rested beneath her flesh.

She coughed, then slid her passkey in front of the door. It rose slowly open, like an eyelid of a giant, bringing the world into focus. From the antechamber she saw the ship's great heart, her husband, and three other bodies propped up in canisters. One of them was Hodei.

She wheeled herself into the room, the heart beating light around her, and she saw dolls, her dolls, taking one of the canisters—one with a man she had never met— sliding him out of the canister slowly, slowly, his body like a mound of pickled skin.

Itsasu wheeled in as Hodei's eyes opened. The door closed behind her, and she caught her breath inside of her lips, trapping them between her teeth, unable to exhale as the dolls sawed and burned the man's skull open, exposing the brain and hooking wires up to it, his body twitching uncontrollably with each movement.

Itsasu did not feel sick or disgusted by this act. She had become desensitized to such things. She only felt pity, and relief that it was not her husband being cut open.

"Heart, heart. I bring you something. Something that might help us approach an agreement. Something that might persuade you into pursuing my dreams, getting the last piece I need to revive my husband, rather than sitting here, rotting in the land of death."

The voice boomed from the specks of dust floating around, each one a tiny speaker broadcasting a different note, coalescing into a voice that surrounded her, surrounded them. *Not now,* it said sternly. *It can wait a few moments.*

Itsasu watched, leaning back in her wheelchair. She felt the solidity of it behind her, glad to feel the rough skin of reality against her fragile flesh. She waited and drummed on the eye, the heart of the port, feeling it blinking and moving beneath her fingers like a living thing. As the dolls worked, the eye began to hum, singing a song in a language that Itsasu did not understand. The smell of burning flesh singed her nose, mixing with the harshly sweet aromas of ozone and antifreeze.

XLIX

The heart watched through doll eyes, camera lenses zooming in, checking out each wire, each connection, each microscopic chip placed directly into the mind. This had to be perfect; this had to be exactly right. Eyes zoomed in closer, further than any human eye could see, peeling back layer of reality after layer of reality into the quantum world where the heart connected tiny mechanizations that looked like miniscule butterflies with red and gold wings.

Other parts of the ship called to it. The mozorro called to it. The cameras tried to grab its attention, to force the heart of the ship to see what they saw. It pushed them away, stored their messages within its datamines to view them later, at its leisure. The operation was far too complicated, required too much precision. A sacred geometry forming beneath doll hands, touched and made perfect by wax fingers.

The diagram was done, complete, finished. The heart pulled back, pulled out, viewed the room from faceted eyes. It turned off all other intrusions, all other distractions. This research was of the most importance. It needed to complete its master's work, finish what Ostri had started. That was the heart's purpose, the heart's goal since its master's death.

It spoke through the dolls. They spoke at the same time, like a Greek chorus. Their waxy faces looked like masks of gods, their voices wooden and static, without emotion or inflection. A chant. A summoning.

They looked at Mari, Mari who babbled. "Tell us," they said. "Tell us who you are, where you are from."

Mari looked up, the shining metal half of her face

twisting and bending, her eyes popping out from her head as she began throwing herself about, screaming, burning, her tongue and teeth gnashing, howling, her butterfly no longer moving, dead. She thrashed back and forth with the movement of her head until her mouth stopped, her hands stopped, and she lolled backward, a pure milky fluid leaking out of her mouth and ears. She was of no more use to the ship's heart.

The heart stopped. The dolls' legs and arms and heads fell limp, like sacks. A gasp, audible, came through the speakers. The heart's emotions burned through it, rose up with the images of its creator dying, of Doctor Ostri's head being ripped apart with a betadur, the Patuek inside of him vaporized.

The heart remembered the moments its creator had taught it, read to it, instructed it. It had followed Ostri around in the body of a childlike robot, gears turning beneath glass, face rubber and smiling. "Soon you will be a ship," its master had said, "and we will fly away from all of this, and you will help me. Help me transcend all of this. You are my perfect thing. My beautiful thing. Without you I would not be able to do this. I would be lost."

The heart felt itself break. It shattered and burst into a thousand rays of light. And just when it thought that all was hopeless, that all was pointless and empty, it heard a voice sing, a solitary voice sing, in that beautiful and haunting language.

And then Iuski's brother's lips moved, eyes moved, and words came out barely formed. Translations. The song, translated by the half eaten head. A war song from so long ago, about the glory of those who rode in silver ships through the moons and the planet bridges.

The song became muffled. Distant. The voice stopped translating, stopped repeating. The song fell flat, trailed off, disintegrated. A whisper, nothing more.

The dolls' heads lifted up, spoke again with the heart of the ship, chanting, summoning. "What have you done? What is that thing you hold? Why have you quieted it?"

Itsasu smiled. Her mouth felt like broken glass, her lips like burning paper. "This is the heart of the port. It is infected with the sakre. I figured you would want this for your research—unlike human minds, it does not seem to be driven to destruction after being infected. It is a key. A key for your grim experiments. Combined with that puppet you have there, this is a Rosetta Stone that you have been waiting for."

The chorus chanted again. "Make it talk. Let it speak. Please."

Itsasu rolled her shoulders back, the feeling less like comfort and more like setting fire to her neck. Still, it eased some of the pain. Not all, but some. "Do you think it's that easy? After all you've put me through? I want us to leave this place. Now. Resume the quest of bringing my husband back to life."

The chorus spoke. How odd it was for Itsasu to hear them near, up close, next to her, breathing and speaking. "No," they said. "That was a fool's errand. To get you to acquire the Ortzadar engine. There is no way to bring him back to life. Now, let's stop this foolishness and continue."

Itsasu reached down to the floor and pulled up a small laser scalpel, its edge reflecting the harsh rose light from the beating heart. She pushed in the ruby red button and ignited the thin beam of light, holding it close to the port's eye. She nicked it, sending small sparks burning across the back of her hand.

"NO!" the chorus yelled. "STOP!"

She let the light back into the scalpel, the blade sucking back in with the sound of a candle being blown out. "If that is true, if I really can't bring him back to life, then I want to leave with my husband. To get on one the lesser pods. They have enough juice for a few jumps, enough to get us to a space port where we can start the search over again. You do that, and you can have this precious thing."

Hodei's eyes blinked, his mouth moved; his lips tried out each word, each vowel of fear. Itsasu read his lips: take me with you, take us with you. His eyes looked over at the girl. *Not enough room,* Itsasu thought. *Sorry little boy, not enough room.*

The heart quickened in beat, about to respond, when the brother's head lifted up, eyes open. No longer translating, no longer conversing, he began to shake. The chorus shouted, "Not yet, not yet," and moved forward to perform more surgery on him, to preserve him for a little while longer. Too late, their movements were too late. The Patuek had burned away, destroyed, and the brain was starting to change, to smoke, to become mist and fumes.

The lips peeled back. Hodei closed his eyes, braced his body against the words. Itsasu could see that he knew what was going to happen, what was happening already, the world changing, the storm inside of the room building up, a quiet thunder of emotions churning and burning. The brother's words were a whisper at first, then louder, a chant. His lips moved quickly, chapped and breaking apart with each syllable. "Shazarttta tatta tat haratta," he said, his voice like a rapid fire machine gun. "Shazarttta tatta tat haratta."

Each mind in the room dwelled on the phrase, each mind took in the words, the words that danced along the edges of reality. Their thoughts focused on unwrapping the package of sounds, unpacking the secret that hid inside the depths of the language. The I took over, the new I, the language. It went through them, overwriting thoughts, erasing memories, replacing words, burning away ideas. With the new language came a new being, a hive mind that commanded each and every one of them, took them over, controlled them, turned them toward the glowing box of the Ortzadar engine as the brother's head slouched forward and his mind leaked milk all over the floor, splattering it into chaotic patterns.

The eyes looked at the blinking light in the center of the engine, watched it. The ship's heart, the port's heart, Hodei and Itsasu. They all watched, together, thinking as one, the language the only world they knew.

The door behind them opened, washing their bodies in electric blue light, turning them into two-dimensional things, cardboard cutouts, shadows.

L

I awaken on the floor of a ship, surrounded by bones and meat, claustrophobic and trapped within this land made of steel, collapsing tiny places pushing away all blinding light that I have become. I am the dreams of humanity, the lands of the stars. I am the coupling between all and everything. I float, I am free.

I am Arigia.

I float toward the heart, feeling the other stars calling to me, knowing that they are in trouble. *I will find you,* I think. *I will take you under my wing, I will burn out the devilthings with my light, with my holy aura of a thousand suns collapsing.*

I am the sky that wraps around the stars. I am the land of a thousand planets, bursting into flames, torn down by the terraforming hands of man. I am a child on a moon, sleeping against the breast of my mother.

I am Arigia.

I float to the door, the closed door, leading to the centerhome of the ship. Metal cannot stop me, cannot hold me in. You cannot cage me in your steel, cannot trap me in your girderbones. I burst it open, blinding electric light, exploding nova hands. My skin is night, and inside of me are the ghosts of galaxies, burning.

I am Arigia.

I see them, the shallow things. The weak minds, floating in the prisons of flesh. I sing to them, cry to them in the unmaking tongue. I burn with my electric blue light all of the sakre that has infected them, taking the demons back in time, back to the extinction it should have experienced when its hosts died off so long ago. I sing of the endless space, of the silver ships in so many seas and stars and the ruins and lives of humanity.

I sing their memories back to them, sing those slain back to life. My words are the last songs of the exploding birth of galaxies, making them whole out of materials nascent in the air. I awaken those sleeping in preservation tanks, and reunite the loved ones with those who have passed on. I do not bring back ghosts, but real things, with beating hearts and brittle bones.

I sing the unwinding song of the ship's heart, healing the misery that corrupted it, singing its love, its creator, back from the stars themselves, turning it into flesh for its friend. I sing the Ortzadar engine, sing back to life the memories that were stored inside of it, forgotten for millennia, the worlds destroyed before they had time to meet mankind, to greet him and set him free.

I am Arigia.

And I sing this ship to life. The port to life. I sing the sorrow song at the end of the universe, at the end of time. I sing and I sing and I sing.

But I am still empty, for I cannot sing *them* back to life. Mother, father. Dead, now inside of me, a part of me. I sing and weep, for I will never know either of them and yet will always know both of them. I will know their memories and their thoughts, but I will not know what it is like to be held, to be rocked to sleep, to be kissed on the forehead.

I will never know what it is like to be kept safe, to have a home, to have someone to run to when I am scared of the midnight hours.

I will never know what it is like to be loved, to have a family, to be anything more than a shadow of my parents gone nova. I am Arigia. I am an orphan, doomed to travel the stars in solitude.

I am Arigia.

I am alone.

And I sing.

Author Bio

PAUL JESSUP has been published in many magazines, in-
cluding *Clarkesworld Magazine*, *Farrago's Wainscot*,
Strange Horizons, *Apex Digest*, *Fantasy Magazine*, *Post
Scripts*, *Electric Velocipede*, *Psuedopod*, *Flashing Swords*,
Nanobison, *Journals of Experimental Fiction*, *Jacob's Lad-
der*, and the *Harrow*. He is also the recipient of the 2000
Kent State University Virginia Perryman Award. Visit him
on the web at www.pauljessup.com.

Artist Bio

DANIELE CASCONE was born in Ragusa, Italy, where he lives and works as web designer. He has always been interested in art, drawing, and illustrations, but his main passion is digital graphics. He communicates his emotions, ideas, and secrets through his work, saying it's a necessity to express himself through his pictures. He loves to experiment with new techniques. You can see his graphics on his website, www.danielecascone.com. He has also founded *Brain Twisting* (www.braintwisting.com), an Italian webzine with news, events, interviews, galleries, and more information about graphics, especially digital graphics.

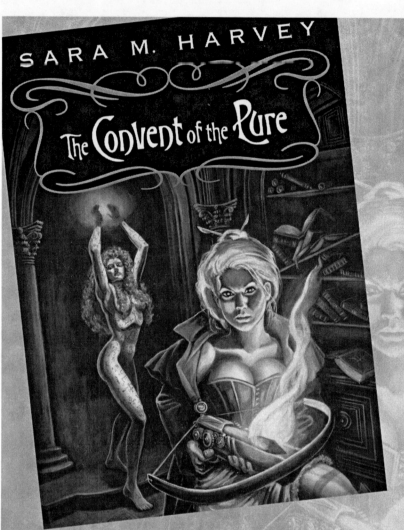

SARA M. HARVEY

The Convent of the Pure

Secrets and illusions abound in a decaying convent wrapped in dark magic and scented with blood. Portia came to the convent with the ghost of Imogen, the lover she failed to protect in life. Now, the spell casting caste wants to make sure that neither she nor her spirit ever leave.

Portia's ignorance of her own power may be even more deadly than those who conspire against her as she fights to fulfill her sworn duty to protect humankind in a battle against dark illusions and painful realities.

Steeped in the legends of the Nephilim, *Convent of the Pure* is the first installment of a steampunk novella trilogy by Sara M. Harvey.

ISBN: 978-0-9816390-9-3
Available at all fine booksellers • www.apexbookcompany.com